WISH I MIGHT

KAIT NOLAN

To everyone who's ever screwed up in love, have hope it can be fixed.

A LETTER TO READERS

Dear Reader,

This book is set in the Deep South. As such, it contains a great deal of colorful, colloquial, and occasionally grammatically incorrect language. This is a deliberate choice on my part as an author to most accurately represent the region where I have lived my entire life. This book also contains swearing and pre-marital sex between the lead couple, as those things are part of the realistic lives of characters of this generation, and of many of my readers.

If any of these things are not your cup of

tea, please consider that you may not be the right audience for this book. There are scores of other books out there that are written with you in mind. In fact, I've got a list of some of my favorite authors who write on the sweeter side on my website at https://kaitnolan.com/on-the-sweeter-side/

If you choose to stick with me, I hope you enjoy!

Happy reading!

Kait

CHAPTER 1

"YOU KNOW HE UP and left Tyler high and dry all those years ago. Broke her heart all to pieces."

"And now he's back?"

"Not only back but playing leading man to her leading lady in the musical."

"No!"

At the tone of utter disbelief from the next booth, Cecily Dixon smiled into her mocha. To her mind, one of the greatest amusements of living in a small town was eavesdropping on the gossip. And boy, were Southerners *champions* at gossiping.

"I thought Tucker McGee got that part."

"He did, but he broke his leg last week. Brody was the understudy. I heard Tyler nearly left the play over it."

"Well, who could blame her?"

For the price of her favorite coffee at The Daily Grind, Cecily got the pleasure of stepping in and out of a series of little one-act plays. Though she'd only been in Wishful for six months, Cecily found that she often recognized the names of at least some of the players mentioned in each tale. And if she didn't, well, she had enough imagination and experience on the stage herself to fill in the gaps, even if she hadn't been in an actual play since college.

Man, she was really going to miss this place.

Her boss, Norah Burke, was the most brilliant marketing mind Cecily had ever known. Following her from Chicago had been a no-brainer. The plan had always been to finish her internship and move on to the best position she could find, as far from her well-intentioned family as possible. To make her mark on her terms. Now that the internship was finished, Norah, the new city planner, was being kind enough to keep Cecily on for hourly wages, while she sent out resumes and interviewed for jobs elsewhere, but there was no full-time position here. That disappointed her more than she'd expected. Mississippi was just supposed to be a stopover. She hadn't expected this tiny, quirky town to get so far under her skin.

She wondered if she'd still be around to find out the resolution of Tyler and Brody's soap opera.

If she didn't get off her butt and get some more resumes out and applications in, she certainly would be. Her personal savings, plus the hourly wage, was enough to get her through the end of the year, but anything beyond that would force her to dip into funds dedicated to other things. She preferred not to violate that particular personal rule if she could help it.

Another pair of women reached the top of

the stairs, bringing with them a new story.

"—there's been some support, but just not enough." The woman's not-quite-put-together look of yoga pants and denim jacket, hair bundled into a messy knot with what appeared to be a pair of pencils, was capped off by the extra-large coffee clutched in both hands. She and her companion sat at the booth behind Cecily.

"I thought for sure the idea would take off after you saved the Booster Club pancake breakfast with your biscuits."

"That helped. And, in fact, it was Ginger Arnold who suggested I try opening a business. But I don't think enough people in Wishful even know about the Kickstarter."

Cecily's ears perked. A local Kickstarter? That was right up her alley.

"There has to be a way to get the word out better."

"I don't know, but I've got to figure something out. Rick's going to be in physical therapy for months, and the doctors have already said he's not going to be able to go back to work at that job. I'm the one who has to step up and be primary breadwinner now. If the Dixieland Biscuit Company doesn't get funded, I don't know what I'll do. I'm a *housewife,* Lucy. I've got no work experience past the waitressing I did in high school."

"There's still a week left to the Kickstarter. Don't give up hope yet."

Cecily opened a new tab on her laptop and hit up the Kickstarter website, doing a search for Dixieland Biscuit Company.

Ah, here we go. Dixieland Biscuit Company, proposed by one Beth Carmichael. As starters for a new business went, it was a modest campaign. The goal was only $15,000, going primarily toward commercial ovens, supplies, and necessary conversion of the proposed business space. But with just over a week remaining, she was sitting at $6,350. That would hardly get it done.

One of Cecily's tasks working for Norah

was managing the city's social media feeds. They'd built quite the connected network over this past spring, when Norah went head-to-head with GrandGoods, the big warehouse store that had tried to come into Wishful. Cecily couldn't think of a single reason not to use it to help Beth start her business. Keeping local business local and revitalizing the local economy was what Norah was all about.

As Lucy and Beth continued to chat behind her, Cecily put together a quick social media blitz, nabbing pictures of the mouthwatering buttermilk biscuits from the Kickstarter page and crafting specialized messages for Facebook, Twitter, and Instagram. She was just getting things laid in and scheduled as her roommate slid into the booth beside her.

"And how are you this fine day, my dearest darling?"

Cecily shot a glance at Christoff, whose usual acerbic wit had sweetened since their arrival in Mississippi back in the spring. She knew the credit for that went to Daniel Palmer, the barista who'd captured his heart.

"Someone clearly just saw his sweetheart."

Christoff grinned, his sharp blue eyes twinkling behind the square-rimmed hipster glasses. "Speaking of, Daniel sent this up for you." He handed over a cookie the size of a bread plate, studded with chocolate chunks and walnuts.

Cecily took a nibble and sighed. "He's adorable, thoughtful, and has amazing abs. *Why* couldn't he play for the other team?"

"Because that's way too much fabulous to pack into a straight man frame. What are you working on here?"

"Just a quick little side project." She finished setting up the multi-point blast for the biscuit shop and clicked back over to the Kickstarter page, logging into her own account. She input her own donation, toggling *Anonymous* before hitting enter and shutting down.

Christoff went brows up.

Cecily just sipped her coffee as a cell phone dinged somewhere behind them.

A mug clattered against a table. "Oh my God."

"What's wrong?" Lucy asked.

"This can't be right," Beth said.

"What? What is it?"

"Someone just donated *five thousand dollars* to the Kickstarter."

"Seriously?"

"Oh my God! I have to go tell Rick!" Beth scrambled up and bolted for the stairs.

"Wait for me!"

Christoff waited until the two women had departed. "You know, I've seen you play a lot of roles over the years, but simple intern has to take the cake."

"It's not a role. I *am* a simple intern. Or I was before I finished the internship."

He kept his voice low. "You are the only trust fund baby I know who insists on living off what you can earn yourself and puts all your inheritance to charity."

She shot a look around to make sure nobody was listening and dropped her voice even lower. "I'm the only trust fund baby you know, period. And you know you're supposed to keep that under your hat."

"Yeah, about that."

Cecily straightened in her seat, grabbing hold of his arm. "Did you tell Daniel?"

"No. Though even if I had, he wouldn't spread your little secret. It's just that the rest of your family seems less intent on letting you maintain your cover."

"What are you talking about?"

Christoff pulled a magazine out of his interior coat pocket and laid it on the table. The latest issue of *M & S*. With a picture of her grandfather smack dab on the cover.

"Oh God." Cecily's hands fumbled as she flipped through to the article. Ten full, glossy pages, complete with family pictures. Including her. "Oh God."

She skimmed the interview. The focus was, as usual, on the family's diversified empire, with plenty of nods given to their charitable foundations and the fact that the family hallmark was investment in people. The bulk of the article talked about her grandfather, her mother, and uncles, including speculation on whether her Uncle Hugh was going to finally enter the gubernatorial race.

"'Intriguingly absent from our interview was the next-generation heir apparent, Genevieve's daughter, Cecily Dixon, a graduate of Brown University and Northwestern, founder of The Hero's Help Alliance.' Oh my God. I am *not* the heir apparent."

"You're the eldest grandchild. Stands to reason that at some point you are."

"No." Cecily shook her head vehemently. She might have been considered on that track once, but she'd blown it. "No. No. No. No. That's not who I am. That's not what I *want*. You *know* how hard I've worked to keep myself separate from all this. I can't let this get out. I don't want people looking at me differently. And the last thing I need is a repeat of

Jefferson. Once was enough, thanks very much."

"Sweetie, if anybody who even vaguely resembles the likes of Jeff the Jerk comes sniffing around you, you can be sure that I, as your trusty pit bull, will slice his balls off."

"I do love you. But I'm serious. We have to round up every copy of this magazine in town." She shoved her laptop into its satchel.

Christoff gave her the Eye. "You know that means you actually have to *go* to the bookstore, right?"

Inglenook Books. The place she'd been studiously avoiding for the last three months because she couldn't bear to see its proprietor. What exactly would *he* think of her suddenly showing up in his shop? Cecily cringed. "You could go for me."

"I was just there, which is where I got *this* copy, and it would look pretty damned weird if I went and bought up all the rest."

Reaching out for his hand, she put on her best begging face. "Christoff, in the name of all our years of friendship, you have to help me with this. Don't make me go in there alone."

He squeezed her hand. "Babycakes, you know I've always got your back."

Cecily relaxed. "Thank you."

"But we're not going in there without a plan. Here's how this is going to work."

"Thank you. Really. I don't know what I would've done if you hadn't been willing to take a chance on hiring me."

Reed Campbell shut the register drawer and looked at his newest employee. In her late thirties, Brenda Walker had just emerged from a vicious divorce, wherein her cheating bastard of an ex had traded her in for a younger model. Stress had whittled her down, and bitterness had carved deep grooves around what might've been a pretty mouth if she smiled. She had no retail experience to speak of, having spent the duration of her marriage as trophy wife to a cardiologist, but she knew books. An avid reader and long-time customer of Inglenook well before Reed bought the place, Brenda had been a familiar face as long as he could remember. She'd worked on a number of literacy campaigns with his mother over the years. Offering her a job had seemed like the obvious and kind thing to do, even before his mom started pressuring him to do it.

A good thing, too, as there was no chance of saying "no" to Anita Campbell.

"You're a smart woman. You'd have figured something out."

"Yes, well, I'm grateful to you that I don't have to." Brenda did smile then, and something about that curve of lips and the tone of her voice had a wisp of unease blooming.

Surely, she wasn't *flirting* with him?

She laid a hand on his arm, her thumb lightly stroking the underside of his forearm. "It's nice to know that there are still some kind men out there."

Nope. He wasn't imagining it. Brenda was actually coming onto him.

Shit.

Reed resisted the urge to jerk away. The last thing he wanted to do was hurt her feelings or shatter whatever nascent confidence she'd managed to rebuild in the wake of her divorce. But he had to shut this down in a hurry. What could he do? What could he *say* that wouldn't embarrass them both?

The door chime sounded, and Brenda's hand fell away as they both turned toward it.

Saved by the bell.

All thoughts of his cougar problem evaporated, replaced by surprise as the woman stepped through the door.

Razor sharp wit, brilliant mind, and geek-tastic sense of humor, all wrapped up in effort-less class. Cecily Dixon. The one who got away.

With a population of only a little over five thousand, Wishful was small enough that they ran into each other often—at the coffee shop, at McSweeney's Market, on the town green. Since her boss was about to marry Reed's cousin, Cam, he even occasionally saw Cecily at family events. But at no point in the last three months had she deliberately sought him out. So what had brought her in today?

Christoff Bergan, the other Chicago transplant who'd followed Norah below the Mason-Dixon line, came in behind her.

"Back again?" Reed asked him.

"I'm just riding shotgun with the damsel in distress."

Cecily rolled her eyes and crossed over to the counter. When she came straight to him instead of diverting to Brenda, Reed felt a surge of curiosity and hope.

"I need your help."

"Name it." He'd do almost anything to make up for the crap impression he'd apparently left her with back in the summer.

"My cousin's birthday is next week, and I'm not going to make it home for the party, so I want to send a nice care package."

"Okay, what did you have in mind?"

"Well, she's really into comics, but I have no idea what she's read and what she hasn't. And as my knowledge of the subject extends only as far as exactly how many plot holes Chris Hemsworth's abs make up for, I thought I'd consult someone who was rather more of an expert."

Reed felt his lips twitch. "I can't decide if that was a compliment or an insult to both my abs and my level of pure geek."

"You can talk pure geek when you can quote the entirety of *Pitch Perfect,* including all the music and choreography—"

"—while under the influence of a pitcher of strawberry daiquiris," Christoff added.

Reed lifted a brow.

"Yeah, that happened." Cecily shrugged and dropped her gaze to his stomach, as if she could see through the button-down he wore. "Anyway, I'm pretty sure your Captain America board shorts were a compliment to both abs and geekdom."

He flashed back to summer, to the feel of

her hand trailing up and down his chest as they lay by the lake, watching the stars and lightning bugs come out.

"So maybe you could channel some of your natural Steve Rogers and help a girl out?"

Reed blinked, coming back to the now and hoping she meant post-super serum Steve. Putting on his best Chris Evans impression, he said, "Happy to help, ma'am. Right this way."

He led her over to the wall of comics and graphic novels. "Tell me a bit about your cousin."

"She's turning seventeen. She's brilliant and independent and stubborn and fierce in the best possible way."

"So she's your mini me."

Cecily cut her eyes to his, a faint wash of pink staining her cheeks. "She also towers over me by a good five inches."

"What you lack in stature, you make up for in personality."

She flashed a rueful smile. "Yeah, let's go

with that. Anyway, I'd love to introduce her to something new and awesome."

"Well, if I was going for new and awesome, with fantastic art, and a serious showcase for strong women, I'd give her this." Reed reached past her to grab an issue off the shelf.

Cecily sucked in a quiet breath, drawing his gaze to her mouth. He'd only kissed her once—a languorous exploration that'd slid a long-running flirtation into serious *what the hell had taken him so long.* Looking at those glossy, pink lips, he wanted to do it again. Did she still taste like honeysuckle?

Reed realized he was all up in her space, but before he eased back, he shifted toward her, just a little. She didn't move back, and her dove gray eyes dilated before they dropped to his mouth.

Not disinterest then. Whatever had gone wrong between them hadn't been about lack of attraction. Reed filed that away.

"*Dark Defenders* is a noir style comic with a lady hero. She's kind of a '40s vigilante—think Agent Carter meets Batman. She has a small support team a la Team Arrow, including a detective in the local precinct, who she saves from getting shot by the big crime boss."

"Please tell me there's a will they/won't they almost romance."

Is that what this is? "Naturally. It's an indie published comic by S.J. Wayfield that's been taking the comic world by storm. But it's pretty new, so unless your cousin keeps up with the cutting edge, she probably hasn't read it."

"Works for me."

"You want to just grab the first issue for her to try or the first collected volume? That's the first eight."

"Volume."

"Excellent choice." Reed grabbed the relevant volume, and they headed for the register. "So, how's the job search going?"

"It's…going. I've had a few interviews, but nothing that I really want."

He sensed reluctance rather than disappointment under that statement. She loved Wishful. He knew she did. And that gave him hope that maybe, just maybe, she wanted to stay. If she did, if she *could,* he might get another shot.

"Well, good luck. I'm sure the right thing will come along. Brenda, you want to take this one?"

"Sure." Brenda offered up a genuine, if rusty, smile.

Reed kept an eye on the transaction, but she rang up the purchase with no problems. She'd be fine on the register while he did some work on inventory.

Cecily lifted her bag in salute. "Thanks for the recs. I'm sure Blair will love them."

"Happy to help." If he asked her out right now, what would she say? He still hadn't sorted out what had gone wrong. Better to think things through before acting.

When they'd gone, Brenda shook her head. "So strange."

On his way back to the tiny room that housed his office, Reed paused. "What is?"

"Her friend just bought out every copy of this month's *M & S.*"

"Really?" That *was* strange. *M & S* wasn't one they usually sold out of, certainly not days after release. And Christoff had already bought a copy the first time he'd come in. "Weird." Making a mental note to order more, he retreated to his office to hide from the cougar on the prowl.

CHAPTER 2

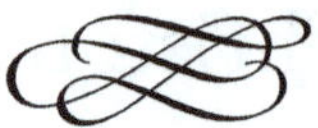

*W*E HAVE HIGH HOPES *for her,* *Cecil reported of his granddaughter.*

Cecily picked up her wine and took another hefty swig as she continued to read the article. Her grandfather knew how to talk the talk. He'd never say anything to besmirch the family name, which meant pretending like The Incident had never happened, like Cecily hadn't screwed up and cost them a small fortune, and as if she were still actually a contender for doing anything legitimate in the family empire.

Cecily knew better. She knew how to read

between the lines of what her family never said and had banished herself before they were forced to sort out the best way to deal with her and the embarrassment she'd caused.

She'd never imagined she'd fall in love with the work she was doing. Or that she'd find an incredible freedom in leaving behind the family name and all its attendant pressures. She was *happy* in the life she was making for herself, even if that life was in transition.

Someday she'd prove herself. She'd make up for youthful mistakes. And then…well, then they'd see.

But someday wasn't here yet and having this publicity out there threatened to undermine everything she'd accomplished. At least the author hadn't unearthed details of The Incident. Or had been discouraged from printing them. None of her Google Alerts had popped to indicate that anybody else was regurgitating that mess again, so chances were, she was safe from anybody in the media sniffing out her current location.

She tossed the copy she was reading onto the small mountain of others littering their coffee table.

"What are you going to do with all of them?"

Cecily glanced at Christoff over the rim of her wineglass. "I have no idea. It's chilly out. Maybe we'll have a bonfire, roast some marshmallows. Make a few s'mores."

"There are probably carcinogens in the ink or paper or something."

"And there aren't in the processed components of s'mores?"

"I feel less like graham crackers and Hershey bars are going to kill me." He crossed over and flopped on the other end of the sofa. "So now what? Our recon mission was successful. Your secret, such as it is, is safe. And you got your flirt on with Reed without the world coming to an end."

"I did not get my flirt on."

Christoff lifted one sardonic brow. "Please." He affected a higher pitched voice and batted his unreasonably long lashes. "'Maybe you could channel some of your natural Steve Rogers and help a girl out?' Lie to yourself, if you must, but don't lie to me. I could practically smell the pheromones wafting off the two of you. You're totally still into him. And despite your questionable ditching of him the last three months, he appears to be still into you."

"And? It's a moot point. I'm leaving."

"So you keep saying. But I don't know why you won't let yourself have a little fun before you go."

"I am not falling into bed with Reed Campbell just for a little fun," Cecily protested.

Christoff's mouth quirked into a wicked grin as he leaned toward her and stole a sip of her wine. "I never said anything about falling into bed with him. I see that lone kiss this summer has inspired all *sorts* of fantasies."

It didn't seem wise to mention she'd had the fantasies *before* the kiss. They'd just gotten infinitely hotter after. And so what? That's all they'd ever be. Fantasies. Despite the undeniable attraction between them—alive and well, as Christoff had noted—she and Reed were fundamentally incompatible. If today's bookstore mission had added a new variation to those unfulfilled fantasies that involved being trapped between that long, hard body of his and a bookcase, well, that was the price she'd have to pay for keeping her secret.

Cecily snatched the glass away and shoved him back with one foot. "You're reminding me why I prefer to live alone."

"With your denial. And without my very excellent falafels."

He really did make amazing falafels. "My denial is perfectly happy with take out."

"It's because it's been so long, hasn't it? I mean, the closest thing you've had to a relationship since The Incident is making it to dessert after dinner. How long has it been since you've had any action?"

Cecily winced.

Christoff straightened. "Please tell me that Tony-award worthy performance with Pierce wasn't the closest you've gotten."

When Norah had been fired from Helios and blackballed by the firm, Cecily and Christoff had concocted an insane plan for Cecily to pretend to seduce Norah's ex—son of the head of the firm—in order to get his admission on camera that Norah hadn't actually done any of the things she'd been accused of. It had worked. Norah had gotten her reputation back and both Cecily and Christoff had turned in their letters of resignation before making the trek to Mississippi to deliver the news in person to the best boss they'd ever had. That they fell into work here had just been icing on the cake.

"Darling, that's beyond sad."

Cecily shrugged. "Precedence indicates I have crap judgment in men." It was hard to trust anybody without wondering what they wanted to use her—or her family or money—for.

"So, you had a bad experience. Did it ever occur to you that you're just as crappy at recognizing the good ones as you are at failing to recognize the bad?"

"Should I take this as a renewal of your campaign for me to let you run my love life?"

Christoff had been on and off that train since high school.

"Which one of us is blissfully happy right now?"

"Oh please. You found Daniel by sheer, dumb luck. It had nothing to do with your being a superior judge of character or having any kind of woo woo matchmaker skills."

"I like to think it was Fate. If not for you, I'd never have come to Mississippi in the first place, and I certainly wouldn't have stayed. I'm just saying that if you won't trust your own judgment, trust mine. You're wrong about Reed."

"So you've been saying for three months. And why does it even matter, Chris? I'm leaving. The job is over."

"If you're so set on leaving, then why have you been so precious and picky about where to go next? You've had offers. Decent ones. And you've turned them down."

Because I'm holding out for a position worthy of a Davenport.

"I'm being picky because I can afford to be. I'm not out to be a cog in a machine somewhere. I'm out to make a mark."

Christoff just shook his head. "Must be lonely up there on that high horse."

Cecily bristled. "I'm not up on a high horse. I'm just—"

"Trying to live up to the expectations you've ascribed to your family, even though you've more or less cut yourself off from all of them." He shoved up and headed for the kitchen. "You need to make a choice, sweetie. Be a Davenport or be normal. Because this whole in between thing you've been rocking the last few years isn't working for you."

He wasn't wrong. But there had to be some kind of middle ground. She'd been trying to walk that line without much success. And it was lonely.

Because no matter what she did to distance herself from her origins, at the heart of it, she'd always be a Davenport, and she'd always wonder if anybody would be able to see her as just Cecily.

"I'D HOPED it was just a one-time thing, but it's been a week, and she's still coming onto me." Reed tipped back his Corona and shuddered. "It's…weird, y'all. And I don't know what to do about it."

"Just tell her you're not interested." Eli Hamilton, king of stating the obvious, dug a chip into the guacamole at the center of the table tucked into the corner of Los Pantalones. The Mexican cantina was actually named Vaquero, but years ago, all of the neon cowboy on the sign had burned out, except for his pants. Nobody knew who'd started the nickname, but it'd stuck.

"All that time spent in the woods away from people has given you the sensitivity of a bulldozer, little brother." Leo, the elder of the twins by ten minutes, merely lifted a brow when Eli flipped him off. "Classy."

"And yet, I'm not the one who's single." He shot a grin and a wink at his girlfriend, who sat on the far side of the restaurant with her friends. Jessie blew a kiss back.

"Any day now, Jessie is going to wake up and realize what a Neanderthal you really are and drop your ass. In the meantime," Leo turned back to Reed, "couldn't you say something to the effect that personal involvement with employees is against company policy?"

"For one, I don't want to draw attention to it at all because that'd make us *both* feel even more weird about it. For another, I wouldn't put it past her to point out that I'm the boss and I make the rules, so I could change them." He could just imagine being trapped in the tiny office with Brenda between him and the door, those perfectly manicured nails hooked around his arm like talons.

Zach Warren refilled his glass from the

pitcher of Corona. "You're overlooking the obvious solution."

"I'm not going to fire her. Do you know what kind of fight that would lead to with my mother?"

"Your commitment to avoiding confrontation has moved beyond pacifism and into wuss territory," Eli said.

"It's not pacifism or being a wuss. It's being a gentleman," Reed retorted. "Something I *know* your mama tried to train you to be. Not that it seems to have stuck."

Eli made a face.

"If you're finished?" Zach said. "No, you need a girlfriend."

Went for that. Landed flat on my face.

Cecily hadn't been back by the bookstore, leading him to conclude she really had just been shopping for her cousin, not out to renew some flirtation with him. He wondered if Blair liked *Dark Defenders.*

"There aren't exactly any real candidates in that department at the moment. And I'm not going to start dating some woman with the express purpose of getting Brenda off my back. It wouldn't be fair to lead somebody on like that. Not to mention I don't need my mom to start hearing wedding bells where there are none. Now that Cam's biting the bullet, the entire family has weddings on the brain."

"What about a virtual girlfriend?"

Reed pinned Zach with a look. "Somehow I don't think a blow-up doll or a Buffybot is going to get me out of this jam."

"Not that kind of virtual girlfriend. Geez. I'm talking about Virtual Match."

Eli picked up the pitcher. "Virtual what now?"

"Virtual Match. It's this service where you can basically get an invisible significant other to get people off your back. You get to set up a profile, make up your story, pick a headshot or whatever, and when anybody asks, you have texts and emails that prove their existence."

Reed's interest piqued. "How's that work?"

"They've got actual people on the other side

writing the texts and emails, so you're interacting with a human, not a computer. There are different levels of the service. But think about it. It's perfect. Takes the lie of a long-distance girlfriend and backs it up with actual proof. Then nobody's the wiser, and your cougar backs off without being embarrassed about her crush on a much younger man."

"The man makes a good point." Eli peered down at his phone. "And at this price per month, it's cheaper than an actual girlfriend, that's for damn sure. Look, I'll even sign you up for a gift subscription."

"Seriously?"

"Don't look a gift girlfriend in the mouth," Leo told him. "Having regular female contact has apparently loosened his wallet. Just go with it."

"Oh, what the hell. It's not like I have any better ideas. Fire away."

Over chips and queso, they signed Reed up for the service.

Leo plucked the phone out of Eli's hand to

take his turn. "Okay, so we need to name your girlfriend. I submit that since she's rescuing you from your cougar, she should be named after the real-life alter ego of a superhero."

"I second this motion," Zach said.

"We're doing this by committee now?" Reed asked.

Eli thumped him on the shoulder. "I think it should be Anna Marie after Rogue, since it's a virtual girl who can't touch you."

"Oh, oh, or Jennifer Walters, the She-Hulk, since Reed needs protecting from the cougar."

This time it was Reed flipping Zach the bird.

"No, she ought to be Sue Storm because she's an invisible girlfriend," Leo argued.

"I am not dating a member of the Fantastic Four."

"What about Betsy Braddock? She actually sounds like a real Southern girl," Zach offered.

"Plus, lots of people haven't ever heard of PsyLocke," Eli added. "Less chance of being outed by accident."

"She's going to be my girlfriend," Reed

protested, "so I'm picking. Selina Kyle. Because who better to take on a cougar than Catwoman herself?"

Zach hooked his fingers into claws and pawed the air. "Rowr."

"Selina Kyle it is. Here, pick a selfie." Leo passed over the phone.

Reed scrolled through the gallery of pics, pausing over a few brunettes who vaguely resembled Cecily. No, he'd rather have the real thing or nothing at all. Moving on, he ultimately settled on blonde with Slavic blue eyes and a sassy smile. He hit next.

"Apparently, we get to pick her personality, too."

"Oh, gimme." Zach snatched the phone.

"Remember, this has to be believable," Reed reminded him.

They settled on something basic enough— intellectual rather than cheerleader bubbly— before moving on to customize the story of how he and Selina had met.

"She's a graduate student at Ole Miss, getting her PhD in English. I met her at a reading up at Square Books," Reed said.

"What's she doing her dissertation on?" Leo wanted to know. His thumbs hovered over the phone.

"Gothic novels. Basically, old school horror."

"Seriously?" Eli looked up with interest. "You can actually write about cool stuff like that? I thought English was all about a bunch of boring, dead white dudes."

Reed gave him a pitying look. "Go back to your woods, Ranger Rick."

Leo finished entering the details and hit a button. "Okay. Last detail."

Whatever that detail was faded into the background as Reed caught sight of Cecily standing near the hostess station, scanning the room. Her eyes met his, and she went very still for a moment, as if waiting. He thought about sliding out of the booth, crossing to her and laying his mouth over the lips she'd parted in surprise. Was it his imagination or were her cheeks going pink?

"Dude, how long have y'all been dating?"

Startled by Leo's words, Reed blinked, and the tenuous connection was broken. Cecily began weaving her way through tables, over to Jessie and the rest of her friends.

Idiot. Of course she hadn't come here looking for him.

"It shouldn't be too long or people will want to know why they didn't know," Zach pointed out.

Cecily slid out of her coat and took a seat, reaching immediately for the drink one of them held out.

It should be after the disaster at the lake. Reed forced his attention back to his friends. "Two months. Long enough to have talked and gotten to know each other and decided to date."

A few button clicks later and Leo gave the phone back to his brother. "You are officially off the market."

"I wonder how long it'll take to kick in." Before Reed even finished the question, his phone was buzzing. He tugged it out of his pocket and read the incoming text.

Hey, Tiger. What are you up to tonight?

"Well, I guess that answers that question."

"What'd she say?" Zach asked, craning his head to see.

Ignoring him, Reed thumbed a reply. **Mexican out with the guys. You?**

The answer came back a few moments later. **Up to my eyeballs in dissertation and wishing we were watching a movie and eating popcorn. Extra butter, naturally.**

Jumping into the middle of a conversation with a complete stranger who was supposed to be *not* a stranger was totally weird. *Well, in for a penny,* he thought, and typed in a response.

CHAPTER 3

BY THE TIME CECILY arrived at Los Pantalones, the parking lot was packed. She had to circle twice before finally snagging a space vacated by a pickup truck that'd been polished to a gleam for Friday night out on the town. Starving and tired, she was looking forward to the margarita the girls had ordered her when she'd texted she was leaving work.

Beth was delighted with Cecily's ideas on how to effectively launch The Dixieland Biscuit Company. Norah was pleased, and that was always a nice ego stroke. As Norah got more and more tied up with other aspects of being city planner, more of the straight marketing work for local business owners was falling to Cecily. And that suited her just fine. She enjoyed putting together campaigns for ways to market on a shoestring…creating something from almost nothing. Which was about the budget that most business owners in this economically-challenged town had to work with.

Cecily was still floating on a professional high as she stepped into the busy cantina and began searching for her friends' table. That high shifted to something a lot hotter as she caught sight of Reed Campbell watching her from across the room. She went still, as if by not moving, she'd somehow blend into her surroundings. How could his eyes feel like a caress from thirty feet away? She felt her skin heat, her body pull tight with wanting.

He blinked and whatever strange hold he'd had on her was broken. More than a little unnerved, she sucked in a steadying breath and hurried across to her friends.

"Sorry I'm late."

Avery Cahill held out a margarita with a sympathetic look. "We can go, if you want."

Of course they hadn't missed that little show.

"Don't be ridiculous." Cecily shrugged out of her coat and took the margarita, drinking a tad deeper than she normally would. He'd been on her mind far too much since her foray to the bookstore last week.

"Are you sure?" Jessie Applewhite reached out to stroke a hand down her arm. "I know things have been weird between you and Reed since that weekend at the lake."

"You're making far too much of that." No, she really wasn't. "Reed and I are fine. Wishful is a small town. We run into each other all the time." And every single time, Cecily had to remind herself why she'd walked away. She reached for the chip basket. "So, what are we talking about?"

"Men," Avery said.

Of course they were. "Shouldn't four adult women be capable of passing the Bechdel test and talking about something *else* on a Friday night out?"

"Not when Jessie's looking all googly-eyed at her guy like we're at some kind of middle school dance." Brooke Redding rolled her eyes and sipped at a margarita. "Way better punch than they had in junior high, though."

Jessie turned back to them, feigning insult. "I'm allowed to be googly-eyed."

"According to the Girl Code, she is," Avery declared. "She gets a full three months by default, plus an extra month due to his level of exceptional hotness."

"I cannot argue with his hotness," Brooke admitted. "Who knew working with trees did *that* for a man?"

"Mostly it's just genetics. See exhibit A, the still very single Leo, who shares his DNA." Jessie gestured toward Eli's twin brother.

They all turned to look at Leo, distinguishable from his brother only by dint of shorter hair and a slightly leaner build. But Cecily's gaze skimmed past him to Reed's rangy frame. Tall, with swimmer's shoulders, his brown hair curled a bit at his collar. She didn't think he'd had it cut since summer. As she watched, he leaned forward, apparently in intense debate with Zach about something.

"I'm sure Leo's just fine, but I'm on a man diet," Brooke declared.

Cecily turned back to the table. "A man diet?"

"I've had seriously craptastic luck with the last several guys I've been out with. The dating pool is not that big here, as you well know, and it's shrinking. Leo Hamilton is one of the last unknown quantities out there in our age bracket. I'd hate to go out with him and find out there's no chemistry, or worse, that he's some kind of closet asshole."

"Leo's not an asshole," Jessie assured her.

"Maybe not," Brooke agreed, "but I'd rather enjoy him just hanging out on the horizon as a very pretty possibility than get confirmation he's a frog instead of a prince."

That was an attitude Cecily could get behind. Wasn't that exactly what she'd done with Reed? It was just too damned bad that she'd kissed him. Now there was no erasing that first-hand knowledge that Reed Campbell's poet's mouth knew exactly how to drive her crazy.

She cursed her traitorous body for glancing back at him. *One kiss. It was* one *kiss.* So why the hell couldn't she get it out of her system?

Naturally her friends noticed.

"Now that's a prince I thought for sure would take," Avery said. "I was positive you and Reed would hit it off, or I wouldn't have dragged you both to the lake."

Victims of Avery's less than subtle matchmaking, Reed and Cecily had been invited as the lone singles to a couples' weekend at a cabin up at Hope Springs. According to Avery, a weekend away was just the thing to finally ignite the slow burning fuse of attraction that had been sizzling between them during months of casual flirtation. And she'd been right. That latent spark of fun and humor had burst into something a whole lot hotter. Which was part of the problem. Because then he'd opened his mouth and ruined everything.

There's no such thing as a woman raised in the lap of luxury, who has even the remotest grip on reality. Ivory tower princesses, all of them.

He hadn't been talking about her at all. Cecily understood he'd been badly burned by his ex. But his casual and sweeping indictment proved he could never handle the truth about who she really was. Cecily had no desire to get more attached to him before the inevitable train wreck, so she'd politely but firmly put on the brakes.

She jerked a shoulder. "There's no sense in me starting some kind of relationship when I'll be leaving whenever I land a new job."

Jessie arched a brow. "And that merited avoiding him for the last three months?"

"I haven't been avoiding him."

"Really? So, the fact that you conveniently had other plans or had to work late every time a social occasion came up where he'd be there is just a coincidence?"

Cecily fought the urge to squirm beneath Avery's gaze.

"Why don't you give him another chance, honey?" Jessie suggested. "He really is a good guy."

"I'm not arguing that he's not a good guy." He was one of the best ones she knew, which had made her disappointment all the keener. "He's just not for me." She was saving them both a lot of grief by acknowledging that on the front end. "And, as I said, I'm leaving, so the whole thing is an entirely moot point."

But as the conversation finally turned to other topics, Cecily couldn't resist glancing back toward him and thinking how much she was going to miss this place.

THE NEW ISSUES OF *M & S* arrived on Monday. Reed had almost forgotten about Christoff having bought them all, but the mystery came flooding back as he pulled them out of the box. Since Brenda was manning the register, he paused in the midst of racking the rest of the shipment to look it over. The cover story was about billionaire philanthropist Cecil Davenport. Like the Vanderbilts or Rockefellers, Davenport was a household name—the kind of name that spoke of old money and breeding. People who lived stratospheres above the normal world. But unlike many of his contemporaries, Davenport was more often in the news for the good things he did with his wealth. Reed dimly remembered having read something about an enterprise he'd entered into with Warren Buffet last year. Something to do with trying to correct the latest debacle in public education.

As he studied Davenport's picture on the front of the magazine, Reed couldn't shake the sense that the guy looked familiar. Probably from having seen him on the news. He began to flip through, skimming articles and by-lines, wondering what had prompted Christoff to wipe out the local supply. Reed turned the page and suddenly he knew exactly why Cecil Davenport looked familiar. Because his gray eyes were staring out of the smiling face of…Cecily. Her picture was right there on the page of this national magazine.

"What the hell?"

Reed hurriedly turned back to the start of the Davenport story—a photo essay and interview designed to humanize the man by introducing the rest of his family.

Holy shit. Cecily was Cecil Davenport's *granddaughter?*

Reed tried to imagine her in that privileged, private world and absolutely failed. She was so…*real* and *normal,* without a shred of pretension.

What the hell was she doing in Wishful working for an hourly wage at City Hall? She could be doing…anything…anywhere. And yet she was here, hanging out with the likes of his small town, not giving off a single inkling that she was so much more than a displaced Yankee with a beautiful smile and a brilliant mind. Of course, that was making the gross assumption that the family fortune trickled down. For all he knew, she was having to work to get by the same as anyone else.

Reed started to rack the magazine, then stopped, whipping it back to beat against his thick skull as he realized, with an abrupt clarity, exactly what he'd done to earn her ill opinion.

"You idiot," he muttered.

That night under the stars, after that one, glorious kiss, they'd talked about careers and life. She'd asked him what prompted him to take over the bookstore. And instead of talking about his desire to make it a hub of the community and his pleasure in spreading his deep love of books, he'd talked about how it was a big screw you to Annelise Arrington, his money-worshiping college girlfriend, who'd wanted nothing to do with his small-time, small town life.

There's no such thing as a woman raised in the lap of luxury, who has even the remotest grip on reality. Ivory tower princesses, all of them.

Jesus Christ. Why had he *said* that? He'd needed some giant cartoon cork shoved in his pie hole to save him from his own stupidity.

After rejecting him, Annelise had gone back home to the coast and ended up marrying some Pretentious Playboy the Fourth. Some heir to a beer distributorship or some such. Which Reed knew because they'd been smack dab on the cover of the *Mississippi Magazine* wedding issue two years ago. He'd spent three months being slapped in the face with the image, seriously considering discontinuing the entire periodicals section of the store the whole time.

He didn't love Annelise anymore. The only reason he'd even been thinking about her at all that weekend was because he'd seen an article in *The Clarion Ledger* society pages talking about some political fund-raising gala she was chairing. The sight of her picture had stirred the whole noxious mess back up, reigniting all those feelings that his life was too small, that he was too unworthy. Instead of thanking God that he'd narrowly escaped a miserable marriage, only to be granted the gift of interest from a much better woman, that sense of inadequacy and bitterness had come pouring out.

All he'd done was prove to Cecily that he was small-minded, petty, and prejudiced against the wealthy. Why on earth *should* she think he'd accept her after that?

Looking around his store, with all its meandering rooms flowing one to the next, a small part of him wondered if Annelise had been right on some level. He hadn't turned Inglenook into the fully engaged community hub he'd wanted. Other than expanding their catalog to be more in keeping with the times, he'd changed very little since he'd bought the place. It was a small town bookstore, and he loved it. But it wasn't the *more* he'd envisioned for it.

The phone in his pocket buzzed. He slipped it out to find a text from Selina.

Hey cutie. How's your day going?

Reed glanced instinctively toward Brenda. Zach's plan had worked like a charm. As soon as she'd found out about his "girlfriend," she'd backed off. No confrontation. No awkwardness. Well, not more than a tolerable level, anyway. Thank God.

Because he had no one else to talk to about this, he texted Selina back. **Do you ever feel stuck?**

Selina: **Stuck how?**

Reed: **I don't know. In life, I guess. When I bought the store a few years ago, I had all these plans for what I wanted it to be. Big, huge plans. And I've just been sitting here looking around thinking that I really haven't implemented any of them.**

Selina: **What's stopping you?**

What indeed? Reed hesitated before answering. **I don't know. Maybe fear of failure.**

Selina: **Well, never trying guarantees fail-**

ure. **Wouldn't you rather try and fail than never take the risk? I mean, what's the worst that can happen?**

The worst that could happen? Having reality bear out Annelise's prediction that his vision would never fit in a town like Wishful. Having her be right about *anything* was enough to give him indigestion. But even if it didn't work, what would he really lose? He liked his bookstore exactly as it was. If he tried something and it didn't take, it wasn't as if he didn't like his life and his work. He was still better off without her, still perfectly content with his small-town world.

Reed texted back. **You know what? You're right.**

Selina: **Good for you! So what's your first step?**

The first and most obvious step would be to take advantage of the assets at his disposal. This kind of project was what Cecily excelled at. What would she say if he asked for her help? She'd probably find an excuse to get out of it and pawn it off on Norah. Not that Norah wouldn't be amazing at this. She'd probably even do it as a family favor. But if he was going to take a risk on the one, why not take a risk on the other?

He hadn't fought hard enough to find out what was wrong this summer, and he'd regretted it ever since. If he could convince Cecily to work with him on this bookstore project, then maybe he could convince her to give him a second chance. Reed knew she was looking for jobs elsewhere, knew that his window of opportunity was closing. It was now or never.

Fingers flying, he texted Selina back. **I'm going to ask for help.**

Selina: **Bravo.**

Reed looked down at the stack of magazines still waiting to be racked.

He owed Cecily an apology. But how could he make one without admitting he knew her secret? And she clearly wanted to keep it a secret or she wouldn't have had Christoff buying up all the evidence linking her to her family. Did she even have a cousin Blair? Or had that whole interlude been an excuse to run interference while Christoff made the purchase? Did that mean Christoff knew?

Didn't matter who knew. Either way, Reed needed the opportunity to do some damage control, to prove that he wasn't the narrow-minded, reverse snob he appeared to be. And there was only one person who had the power to give that to him—his cousin's fiancée.

She answered on the first ring. "This is Norah."

"Hey, it's Reed. Have you got a minute?"

"For you I can make two. What's up?"

Reed glanced uneasily at the counter, where Brenda was affixing sale stickers to a pile of hardbacks they needed to move. He didn't want to discuss this here. "Can you meet me at The Grind?"

He could all but hear her curiosity pique in the silence.

"Sure. See you there in fifteen?"

Reed tipped the phone away from his mouth. "Brenda, are you okay to watch the shop on your own for a bit?"

Startled, she looked up. "Sure. It's been pretty slow today, and it's another hour or so until the after-school traffic trickles in."

He spoke back into the phone. "Fifteen."

By the time Reed had stowed the magazines in his office—he wasn't going to be the one to blow Cecily's secret—and walked across the town green, Norah was waiting, a large coffee in one hand, a lemon square in the other. He made his own order, and they retreated upstairs for some privacy.

"I need your help."

"Name it," she said instantly. "Is Inglenook in trouble?"

The bookstore wasn't exactly a cash cow, but it was holding its own. Reed shook his head. "Not in trouble, no. But not living up to its potential, either."

"Color me intrigued."

"This is partly to do with the store and partly a

more…personal matter. And before I go on, I need your assurance that you won't say anything to the rest of the family. Not even Cam. It's a matter requiring discretion." Clearly Cecily valued that.

Her dark eyes sharpened. "Okay, I promise."

"I know you tried to set me up with Cecily."

One elegant brow arched. "I did no such thing. I made introductions between two people I happen to care a great deal about and then stepped back to let nature take its course. Which was apparently nowhere."

Reed winced. "Yeah, well, that's my fault. I said something that left her with a bad impression. And I want the chance to fix it."

The other brow climbed up. "Why now? It's been three months."

"Because I only just figured out what I did wrong."

"Better late than never, I suppose. What does this have to do with me? Why not just apologize to her like a big boy?"

Reed glared. "Because…reasons. It's more

complicated than that." He didn't know if Norah was aware of Cecily's background, but if she wasn't, he wouldn't be the one to break her secret.

"So…you want me to do what, exactly?"

"Get her to work with me. I just need the chance to spend some time with her, so she can see that I'm not… Well, just so she can see me without my foot shoved halfway down my throat."

Norah angled her head and studied him. "You know Cecily's internship is over, right? She's hanging around working hourly for me only until she lands a full-time position elsewhere."

He'd known that objectively. But that was before he felt the flare of hope that he might be able to earn a second chance. "Why can't that be here? Don't you want her to stay? Keep the dream team together and all that?"

"Of course, but we don't have it in the budget to hire her full-time at the rate she merits. She'd have to do something other than work for the city."

"Well, don't you at least want to stack the deck, give her more reasons to stay than go?"

"Do you?"

"I want the chance to try."

"You believe you might be a weight on the side for staying?"

He thought about that flare of desire he'd seen in her eyes at the shop last week and that potent glance they'd shared at Los Pantalones. "I think there's something between us, and we didn't get a proper chance to explore it before I inadvertently screwed things up. I need the chance to make it right."

Norah nodded. "I understand the need for that. I'll arrange for the set up, but the convincing will fall wholly on you, cousin."

"That's all I can ask for." He'd just have to make the most of it.

"YOU WANTED TO SEE m—oooh my God, I'm sorry."

Cecily hurriedly shut Norah's office door, but not before she had a flash of a bare-chested Cam Crawford pressing a kiss to his bride-to-be's bared shoulder. As she stood in the hall, listening to hurried movements on the other side of the door, she couldn't help but think it'd be nice to have someone to be that reckless with. Her brain conjured up an image of Reed.

Bad. Idea.

The door opened and Cam stepped out, fully dressed and pink all the way to the tips of his ears. "Sorry about that. We, uh—"

Feeling the heat in her own cheeks, Cecily waved him off, careful to keep her eyes above the equator. "Almost married and crazy about each other. I get it. Sorry I interrupted."

Norah stepped up behind him, looking considerably less embarrassed, with only her hair remaining a bit mussed. How did she do that? "Someday you're going to remember to lock the door." She brushed her lips over his.

Cam stroked a hand down Norah's cheek in a lingering caress that made Cecily's heart sigh. "See you in New Orleans, Wonder Woman."

Norah stood and watched him, love shining in her eyes, until he was out of sight. Then she straightened and gestured Cecily inside. "You might as well come on in and get the mocking over with."

"Why would I mock? If anything, I'm envious. You two are adorable. And God knows you deserve it after how your ex treated you."

"I won't argue with that." With practiced fingers, Norah twisted her hair back up and secured it with pins. "Just as well you showed up. I need to be getting on the road and he wasn't in any hurry to let me."

Cecily smirked. "You were fighting him off so hard."

Norah flashed a wicked grin. "Come help me haul stuff to the car."

Fifteen minutes later, Cecily loaded the easel and shut the trunk. "That's the last of it. Do you have the PowerPoint?"

"On a flash drive and loaded on the hard drive of my laptop, just in case. I appreciate all your hard work on this presentation. With the dramatic turnaround we've seen in Wishful this year, everybody wants to know how to duplicate our results."

Cecily dimpled. "Do they know they'd best be investing in cloning technology? None of it would've happened without you."

Norah swung an arm around her shoulders. "You either. Who knew this time last year that

I'd be speaking as an expert at a small-town re-development conference?"

"We've come a long way from Chicago. When are you back?"

"Not until Tuesday. Cam's driving down to meet me Friday night, and we're taking a long weekend in New Orleans, so I'm leaving you to man the fort while I'm gone."

"You can count on me!" Cecily gave her a sharp salute.

"I always can." Norah grinned. "Oh, I almost forgot. I promised Reed some marketing services for the book signing he's got coming up at Inglenook. With all the prep for the conference, I haven't had a chance to even look at his stuff, and time's running out. So I'm taking boss's prerogative and dumping it on you while I'm gone."

The smile on Cecily's face turned brittle. "You want me to do the marketing for the bookstore?"

"Cakewalk compared to what you've been doing. It'll be a nice change of pace. He's expecting you sometime today."

As Cecily stared, Norah rushed on, opening the car door and sliding into the driver's seat. "You're a lifesaver. I need to get going. Long drive. See you next week!"

Before Cecily could come up with a viable reason why she couldn't do the job, her boss was driving away.

Crap.

She put it off until after lunch, fortifying herself with one of Mama Pearl's chocolate chip milkshakes from Dinner Belles, the local diner and biggest gossip competitor to The Grind. By then she'd just about convinced herself to put on her big girl panties and get it over with. Procrastinating wasn't doing anything but making her more nervous.

An attractive woman in her late thirties was stocking shelves when Cecily stepped inside the bookstore. She dimly remembered seeing her during the evidence-wiping mission she'd run with Christoff the week before.

The woman looked up and smiled slightly as

Cecily approached. "Can I help you with anything?"

"I'm looking for Reed, actually."

Something flickered over the woman's face —a quick darkening of expression before she seemed to shake herself out of it and reaffix her customer smile. "He's in the back, in his office."

Wondering what that was about, Cecily headed toward the back of the store. In some long-ago lifetime, the building had been someone's home. She wandered through the wide, cased openings, past row upon row of shelves and the comfortable furniture grouped here and there to invite people to sit and stay a while. The overall effect was one of warm welcome. The only thing missing was the scent of baking cookies from the kitchen they might not even have.

As the woman had said, Reed was in his office. She found him at his desk, a pair of horn-rim reading glasses perched on his nose as he peered down at a catalog of some kind. The sleeves of his button-down shirt were rolled up, revealing muscular forearms. The muscles in one of those arms flexed as he made notes with an honest-to-God fountain pen. Something in her brain short-circuited and her mouth went dry. God, the sexy professor look worked on him.

As if sensing her eyes on him, he looked up, brightening. "Cecily. Hey." He pulled the glasses off as he stood, and she felt a pang of regret. "Did she like it?"

Cecily blinked. "Did who like what?"

"Blair. Did she like *Dark Defenders?*"

"Oh." She relaxed against the door frame. "Yeah, she loved it. We're in intense debate about Cass and whether she's good or bad and why she keeps showing up at all the stuff Mena is investigating."

Reed grinned. "You read it?"

"Cover to cover. Impressionable teen and all that. I had to know what I was giving her."

"And what do you think? Good or bad?"

"I think Cass has her own agenda and that

Derrick knows more than he's telling Mena. His reaction is way too vehement."

"Derrick is a pretty straight-forward dude. Very black-and-white. From his perspective Cass is a villain."

"Exactly. So how the heck are he and Mena supposed to work? She's so gray. That's part of what makes her good at what she does. I just don't see how such a straight arrow can be a match for her."

Reed crossed his arms and leaned a hip against the desk. "I think she fascinates him. He's keeping her secret for reasons even he doesn't understand—and that makes for compelling conflict."

Cecily had the strangest sense he wasn't talking about the comic anymore. Which was ridiculous.

"Guess I'll find out more in Volume 2."

He started around the desk. "I'll show it to you."

"Later. That's not actually why I'm here."

"Oh. Then what can I do for you?"

You can stop being so damned appealing.

She steeled her spine. "It's more what I can do for you. Norah's tied up with conference stuff, so she sent me in her stead. My marketing expertise is at your disposal."

"Really? Wow, that's awesome. Nice of you to put in the time."

She could've said something about how it had nothing to do with her being nice and everything to do with her job. But he was being so gracious, she didn't see the point in mentioning it.

"Where should we start? Do you need to know the details of the author? It's Tony Becker."

The name sounded vaguely familiar. "Mysteries, right?"

"Yeah. He's a solid, midlist author. Biggest one we've managed to land so far."

"That's good. If he's given any thought to this at all, he ought to have some kind of press kit we can use. But I'll get into that later. If he hasn't, I can make one. I've done it before." *I can piggy back on what I did for Aunt Dinah. Probably.* She made a few mental notes on what might need tweaking there before turning her attention back to Reed. "But before we get into the specifics, I need to get a better idea of what kind of information dissemination infrastructure you have in place. So, let's start with an assessment of where you are now. Just the basics. Do you have a website?"

"Of course we have a website."

"Show me."

He gestured for her to come behind the desk with him.

The office was tiny, with room only for the ancient wooden desk, a visitor's chair, and a couple of file cabinets shoe-horned in behind the door. In order to get a look at Reed's laptop screen, she found herself wedged shoulder-to-shoulder with him—or more properly shoulder-to-arm, as he was a good eight or ten inches taller than she was. She tried desperately not to notice as his body brushed hers.

"It hasn't been updated in a while, but it's got all the basics on there."

The page loaded and Cecily actually felt faint. Frames. The website was built on *frames.* "Dear God," she muttered. "It's ancient. It's the website that time forgot."

"It's not *that* bad," he protested. "It's got our location and hours. Even a page of events. What more do we need?"

Cecily just shook her head in pity. "Please tell me you've at least got a newsletter."

"Sure. It goes out in the mail once a month."

"*Snail mail?*"

"Um. Yeah?"

"Christ. You're killing me. What about the social media?"

His lips curved in a rueful smile. "I'd tell you, but I'm pretty sure you'll hit me."

She took a deep breath. Which was a mistake because now she could smell his aftershave and felt a ridiculous desire to nuzzle just there beneath his jaw. "Okay. We're just going to pretend you have nothing, and I'm starting from scratch. We'll talk further about what other features you might like once I have the basic framework in place." Before she had more of her brain cells scrambled, she scooted out from behind the desk.

Reed followed. "Thanks, Cecily. Really. This is all way outside my scope of expertise."

"I'll get to work on it this afternoon."

"Why don't you work from here? It'd be a change of pace from the office, and you'd get a feel for the shop and how it fits into the community. Norah's kept you so busy, you haven't really had an opportunity to spend much time here."

Yeah, let's pretend that's the reason.

Still, observing the shop in action over a period of days would give her the opportunity to see what was working for them and what wasn't. She'd know better how to target things with that information.

"Sure."

Reed took her out front and introduced her

to Brenda. "Cecily's going to overhaul our website and stuff."

"If that's what you want to call dragging your business kicking and screaming into the twenty-first century."

"Hey, I'm not screaming."

Cecily couldn't resist a pointed grin. "Yet. Where should I set up?"

He paused, glancing at an incoming text and laughing under his breath before shifting his attention back to her. "Wherever floats your boat. There's better plug access up in the front room, near the graphic novels."

"Sounds good."

She thought maybe he'd hover or come up with some other reason to keep checking on her, but instead he went on about running his business. Cecily felt caught somewhere between relieved and deflated.

Don't be stupid. You made it clear you didn't want to date him. He's respecting that. Just do your job.

An hour into customizing an out-of-the-box

Wordpress theme, the bell chimed and a gangly kid in jeans that had probably acquired the rip in the knee from actual wear came barreling into the store. Excitement was pumping off him so hard, Cecily could feel it from ten feet away. As he rounded the corner, into the room where she was working, she figured there was some awesome new release in comics, and he'd just gotten his allowance. But instead, he made a beeline for the counter.

Behind it, Reed grinned. "Hey kiddo. What's up?"

"I finished the first issue of my comic!"

"Yeah?" Reed shoved a pen behind his ear and set aside whatever he was doing to give the boy his full attention. "Will you show me?"

Intrigued, Cecily shamelessly eavesdropped. The pair of them dropped companionably onto the floor, cross-legged. The boy pulled a sketchpad out of his backpack and handed it over. Reed paged through, reading with the kind of focus he might devote to a best-seller.

"The artwork is fantastic, Austin."

The kid perked up before giving a wary frown. "But?"

"Well, you've created a guy who's a hero straight out of the gate. That doesn't make for a real interesting story. Why are we supposed to root for him?"

Austin jerked a shoulder. "I don't know. 'Cause he's awesome. That's why he's called Captain Awesome."

"But surely Captain Awesome wasn't totally awesome from the get go. Something made him awesome."

"Like radioactive sludge?"

"A classic for a reason," Reed agreed, "but I'm talking about character arc."

"What's that?"

"Well, instead of starting your character out here, think about building him. No hero starts off as a hero. You gotta give your readers somebody they can relate to in the beginning, more their level, who grows into being a hero. Think about Peter Parker. He started out a little geeky dude. Smart but picked on by others. And then he gets bitten by that spider, gets super powers, and suddenly has the skills to start helping people. But even then, he's not automatically a hero. He has the skills, but he helps himself first."

Cecily watched him, head together in deep discussion with the boy, and her heart sighed.

Brenda came to perch on the arm of the sofa, her embittered face softened with a smile. "He's always doing stuff like this."

"Yeah?"

"He's a big softie. Always going out of his way for other people. Can't think of a single other reason he'd have hired me after my divorce. I'm sure there were other more qualified people, but he saw me in a jam and gave me a way out."

Reed Campbell knew the value of investing in people. Except, instead of investing money, he invested his time—possibly a rarer, more valuable commodity. Her family would like him. *She* liked him. It was just too damned bad that he'd never be able to get past the family ties she couldn't escape.

"—I built the site with Wordpress, which is really user-friendly, so I can show you both how to update things once you decide who's going to be responsible for what."

When Cecily glanced up at him, Reed fought the urge to point at someone else in a *Not me* gesture.

"I swear, it's not that bad once you know what's what."

"What kind of stuff would we update it *with?*" Brenda didn't look anywhere near as alarmed as he'd expected. Maybe a challenge would be good for her. And generating website content would keep her focused on work instead of him. She'd stopped outright hitting on him, but there was still a low-level flirtation that made him uncomfortable.

"That's up to you. There's an integrated calendar, which will enable people to add an event to *their* calendar at the click of a button. You could use the blog to share book reviews. In fact, that might be a great way to really make your customers feel like they're a part of things here. Give them a chance to write a guest book review for the store blog. Free content by local people. They'd be proud of what they did and tell all their friends, which gives you word-of-mouth traffic to your target audience."

Reed nodded, seeing the brilliance in that. "I know at least a dozen people who would be all over that. What else?"

The phone in his pocket buzzed. As Cecily named a half-dozen other things that had his head spinning, he slipped it out and read the text from Selina.

What are you up to?

Reed: **Having my mind blown.**

Selina: **Not sure how to take that...**

"— the sort of thing that would be easily cross-posted on all the integrated social media."

Reed's head shot up. "We have social media now?"

"Sure do. And you've already got followers on Twitter, Instagram, and Facebook." She clicked over to show them.

He stared at the numbers. "How?"

"I piggybacked on the city's social media to notify folks in Wishful that Inglenook has entered the world wide web. I've generated enough content to get you through the next two weeks. That'll give you some ideas about the kind of things you can post, and see what sorts of things your clientele is into, and also where they're hanging out. I'm anticipating you'll see the most action on Facebook."

"Okay, Facebook I get." Brenda looked almost excited. "I can deal with Facebook."

Cecily shot her a warm smile. "I've made a list of resources you can use for scheduling content across platforms. You don't want to automate everything, but that way you can drip things into your various feeds at optimized times of day so that there's something going on.

And you'll cruise through a couple times a day to actually interact with your followers so they know you're a human, not a bot."

Reed: **Have you ever met an author or artist who's a master of their craft and had a conversation wherein they make it seem like what they did was easy?**

The phone buzzed again as Cecily began describing some of the other tools they could use to jazz things up.

Selina: **I got to meet Stephen King once. That was pretty cool. And intimidating.**

Reed thumbed a reply. **Well, this is like that, but with marketing. This new plan is going to be great for the store!**

Selina: **I'm so proud you're taking this step!**

He shoved the phone back in his pocket. "Cecily, this is awesome."

She held up a finger. "Not done yet."

"There's more?" What else could there be?

"I've set up a proper mailing list for you, so when you have that newsletter to send out, you can send the same information out to them via email. And there are already fifty-four people signed up."

"Seriously?"

"I've even designed a template to match the design of the website, so everything is neat and branded."

Reed nodded. "Brenda, can I borrow your notebook and a pen?"

With a look of faint surprise, she handed it over to him. He flipped to a clean page and did a quick sketch, being sure to cover his work so neither of them could see. Then he ripped the sheet out, grabbed a binder clip, and stepped over to Cecily. She didn't step back—couldn't because of the counter behind her—and he was aware he'd invaded her space again. She smelled like cinnamon and oatmeal cookies today, and he had to resist the urge to lean in for a taste.

She tipped her head back, looking more quizzical than disturbed, as he reached out to fasten the paper to her collar. "What on earth are you doing?"

"Adding a piece to your uniform." The backs of his knuckles just barely brushed the soft skin of her throat.

Her short, sharp inhale was barely audible. Reed's gaze flicked to hers, holding long enough to see her pupils dilate before he stepped back.

Cecily recovered quickly, looking down at the Superman shield he'd drawn with a big C in the middle. Her laughter rang out, bright as a bell. "I dig it. I'd be quite happy to add this as a formalized part of the uniform."

"You earned it."

"Just doing my job."

"Still. I should have expected it. You *are* Norah's protégée, and everybody knows she's a marketing genius. Clearly the apple doesn't fall far from the professional tree."

She shrugged it off, but her cheeks pinked at the praise. "That *is* why I came all the way from

Chicago to work with her. I'll miss her when I go."

Reed dimmed a little at the reminder. She had plans for her future and they didn't include Wishful—wouldn't, unless he could come up with a way to convince her to stay. "Any luck on the job search?"

"Not yet—"

He held in his fist pump.

"—but I sent out another round of resumes this week. Something will turn up. Anyway, we still need to talk about the book signing. This was all setting up infrastructure to actually *tell people* about it."

The door opened and a babble of voices carried back to them.

"That'll be the book club ladies. I'll go see to them." Brenda headed up front to greet people.

Reed took one of the stools behind the counter and patted the other. "Did you get the press kit I forwarded to you?"

Cecily didn't hesitate before joining him.

"Yeah. It's really bare-bones. Have you read Becker at all?"

"I read his debut. He's not bad. The shipment of his latest arrived a couple days ago, but I haven't started it yet."

"We'll come back to that. How about instead you tell me what your vision is for this place?"

Now was his chance to make up for the poor impression he'd given at the lake. "It's not just a store. Not just brick and mortar and books. I want it to be a focal point in the community. A gathering place. To an extent we already do some of that. Like the book club out there. My grandmother's knitting circle meets here once a week. The high school writers' guild meets here twice a month. But I want to go beyond that. I want to be the next Square Books."

At her blank expression, Reed remembered she wasn't from the area. "Square Books is the independent bookstore up in Oxford. It's a local institution up there, located right in the heart of town. I'm pretty sure I was in there at least every other week for a reading or signing from some author or other, when I was in college at Ole Miss. They do such a great job of community engagement, with carrying on the literary tradition. I want to do that. I want to bring that kind of culture here. Except with a slightly less literary bent because we aren't a university town and that's not our demographic."

She beamed and thumped him on the shoulder. "Look at you using marketing lingo."

"Norah *is* almost a part of my family. I've picked up a little by sheer osmosis."

Her lips curved, her eyes warm as she looked over at him. "You love it. The store. The life you have here."

"I really do."

"It's a good life."

Looking into her face, Reed could see that she really meant it and that she remembered what he'd said all those months ago.

"I like to think so."

"You understand that a town without a

bookstore isn't really a town. That it'd just be fooling itself."

"Not a bad paraphrase from *American Gods.* I didn't know you were a Neil Gaiman fan."

Cecily shrugged. "I read a lot of different things. And I can't say as I disagree with him. Bookstores are important, and I think the fact that you've worked so hard to keep this one going, during a time when independent booksellers across the country are closing their doors, is a very admirable goal."

Reed preferred to believe he didn't need validation of his life choices. He knew what he wanted and intended to go for it, regardless of what anyone thought. But the fact that Cecily understood it, that she admired that choice, soothed something in him. "Thanks."

"It's a real investment in the community. And it's my job to sort out the best means of maximizing that investment of time, effort, and capital. I'm just not quite there yet."

"I guess it's a little hard to imagine if you haven't actually seen it." Inspiration struck. "Actually…you *can* see it. Greg Iles is doing a reading in Oxford on Thursday night. We should go. You'd get a first-hand view of exactly what I'm talking about, and afterward, we could go grab dinner on the Square. You haven't lived until you've had the jalapeno cornbread at Ajax."

She arched a perfectly manicured brow. "Is it really that good?"

Reed laid a hand over his heart and did his utmost to look serious. "Would I lie to you about cornbread?"

She snorted. "I suppose that's a jailable offense down here?"

"Damn straight."

"Fine. I guess it's a date."

He answered her smile with his own. "Guess it is."

CHAPTER 5

"DARLING, I WISH YOU'D just let me make some phone calls—"

"Mom, no," Cecily insisted. "I'm not capitalizing on family connections to get a job."

"It doesn't diminish your achievements. It just opens the door. That's how things work in the business world. You use the connections you have."

Cecily resisted the urge to bang her head against her desk. "That's not how *I* want to work. I'm doing this on my own."

Her mother's frustration was palpable in the

silence on the other end of the phone. "So stubborn," she said at last.

"I come by it honestly from both sides."

"Via multiple generations," her mother agreed. "Fine. But since you haven't yet started a new position, you're free to come home for the gala for the Alliance. We could use your professional expertise to get the word out to prospective donors, and it would be good for you to be seen."

"I'm happy to help with the marketing from here, but coming home for the event is out of the question. Being *seen* is the last thing I want or need." The very idea of facing the cameras and the microphones had a cold sweat breaking out down her back. "And I don't appreciate Grandpa including me in that article in *M & S*. What if somebody dragged up everything that happened all over again? How would *that* publicity look when I'm trying to interview for things?"

"Cecily, we aren't going to pretend like you

don't exist. You are a member of this family, and you've been hiding long enough."

The ring of truth to the statement had her bristling. "I'm not hiding. I've been finishing my Masters degree."

"Which you've done with considerable accolades, and we're proud of you. But you graduated in August at the top of your class. It's halfway through October and you haven't taken another job. You can't tell me you haven't had offers. Is there something else keeping you in Mississippi?"

An image of Reed flashed through her mind. But that was absolutely ridiculous. They weren't together, hadn't been in any kind of relationship. Ever. She wasn't staying for him.

"I'm just…not finished here," she said lamely. There was no way she could adequately explain that to anyone in her family.

A flash of movement in the doorway drew her attention. Norah paused, curled fist hovering over the door jamb. She mimed that she could come back later, but Cecily shook her head and waved her in.

"Listen, Mom, I have a meeting. I need to go. Send me the details on the gala, and I'll work something up, okay? Love to Dad and everybody."

Cecily ended the call a few shades too fast to be considered polite. Then she just laid her head down on her desk.

"That bad, huh?"

"They don't understand why I'm still here. And I can't explain it to them."

Norah shut the door and dropped into the lone guest chair. "Is that because you don't know the answer yourself or because you don't think they'll accept it?"

"Some of both. I feel caught between who I am and who they expect me to be. I know you understand that. You've lived it."

"I have," Norah agreed. "I absolutely know what it is to struggle under the burden of family expectation. And I know what it is to want to forge your own path, either in spite of those expectations or within the confines of them. Mine led me here. To Wishful. To Cam. My parents may not really understand why I do what I do, but I stopped living my life worrying about what they think."

Cecily blew out a breath. "I am so not there yet."

"Yeah, well, I just had my parents' expectations. I imagine having an entire dynasty to live up to is rather a bigger burden."

"That's putting it mildly. Davenports are born for greatness. With a hefty dose of social and civic responsibility thrown in."

"God save us both if my father ever hooks up with your granddaddy."

They shared a mutual shudder.

"Still, in terms of the greatness department, I'd say you've done an admirable job. You're the most talented graphic designer I've ever worked with. No frills, no fuss, just honest truth. I say that as your boss."

"And as my friend?"

"I think greatness is in the eye of the beholder." Norah crossed her legs and fixed those dark brown eyes on Cecily. "You said you weren't finished here. What did you mean?"

"I'm pretty sure I could work with you for a decade and still learn something from you every day. I don't think I'll ever feel finished with that."

"Much as it flatters me that you stayed to learn from me, you're ready to move on and learn from someone else. But I don't think this struggle is about the work. If it was, you'd have been gone by now. Either to one of your family's companies or somewhere else. So what's unfinished?"

Cecily dropped her head back and stared at the ceiling. "I didn't plan for Wishful. I never dreamed when I came down here after Chicago that I'd stay at all. Let alone that this place would get under my skin. I've done good work here. Work that's made a difference. It's incredibly gratifying to know that, when I do go, I've left this town a little better than I found it. I did that entirely on my own merits. Here I'm just

Cecily Dixon. And it's allowed me to keep pretending that I can just be this totally normal girl, that where I come from doesn't matter."

She sat up. "But it does, even when I don't want it to."

"How's that, when you hide who you are?"

She sounded like Christoff.

"Because it's stopped me from making choices, exploring options that I might otherwise have jumped at."

"What choices?"

"You know, when you came back to Chicago and told me what you'd been doing down here, when I saw how incredibly happy you were with Cam, I thought to myself, 'I want to be Norah when I grow up.' I mean, I already wanted to be you professionally, but it just seemed like everything was lining up perfectly for you. I wanted that kind of happy. Do you remember what I said?"

Norah laughed. "You asked if Cam had any single cousins."

"And you told me about Reed. I didn't *actu-*

ally expect to come down here and have your good luck, but it was a nice fantasy."

Norah offered a sympathetic smile. "I'd be lying if I didn't admit I was hoping for that for you too. But that's not what happened. You and Reed never quite connected."

"I didn't let it happen. And believe me, that took some serious work."

Norah frowned. "Why?"

"Because, at the end of the day, whether I want to be or not, I'm a Davenport."

"Okay, promised myself I wasn't going to get involved, but you're going to have to explain that one. You're about as far from a snob as you can get, so I know you don't think he's beneath you."

"No. I think he's smart and funny and gorgeous. My family would love him."

"Is it because his life is here and you think you have to leave to appease your family?"

"That's part of it. But the bigger part is I don't think he can handle who I really am."

"You don't think," Norah repeated. "So you haven't told him?"

Cecily shook her head.

"He said something to stick his foot in it." It wasn't a question.

"That's one way of putting it. And it was fine. Because I'm supposed to leave. Not having emotional entanglements here makes that easier."

"I'm sensing a 'but'."

"But…you threw me to the wolves when you asked me to build his marketing plan."

"How so?"

"Because we've spent all this time together over the past week, and it reminded me of all the things I like about him. I've got all these 'what if's circling in my brain, wondering if I made a mistake holding back these last few months. And now we're going on this business date—"

Norah held up a hand. "I'm sorry. You can have a date or you can have a business function. A business date is not really a thing."

Cecily winced. "It is if you're going to an event together for business research and the evening has date-like overtones."

"What exactly are y'all going to do?"

"Attend a reading at Square Books and then dinner at Ajax."

"Oh, you *have* to try the squash casserole. It's my favorite. And, for the record, nothing about that sounds businessy."

"He wants Inglenook to be the next Square Books, so on that front it is. He wants me to see first-hand what that means. But it's not *just* that. And I don't know what to do about it."

"Do you need to do something about it? You're still going, right?"

"Yes, I'm going. But I'm so conflicted about the whole thing. Part of me wants to be sensible and smart and keep things entirely profes-sional. Because I could land my dream job any day."

"And the other part?"

"He's my unfinished business. If I hadn't put on the brakes in June, I know we'd have been dating. Doing all that get to know each other stuff and figuring out if what's between us is more than just chemistry. If I hadn't put on the brakes, I'd *know* by now whether he needed to factor into my decision about what comes next. But I did put on the brakes, and I don't know if it's smart to start anything with that ticking time clock hanging over my head."

Norah offered a sympathetic smile. "You want my advice?"

"I wouldn't have told you if I didn't."

"Go on your date. Let it *be* a date. And tell him who you are. I know you're worried about discretion and you don't want it to get out. Reed's not the kind to gossip. But tell him and see how he reacts. If you were right, and he can't handle it, then at least you'll know and can move on with a clear conscience and without having gotten further attached. And if you were wrong, wouldn't you rather know it and make up for lost time, however long you're still here?"

Cecily blew out a breath. "I guess knowing

either way is better than second guessing my-self. Can I ask you something else?"

"Of course."

"What the heck should I wear?"

"SORRY ABOUT THE WALK. I didn't realize it was a game weekend." Reed hoped the half-mile hike in those heeled boots wasn't going to hurt Ceci-ly's feet.

She looped her arm through his and smiled. "I don't mind. It feels good to stretch my legs, and it's nice to see a little more of Oxford. I've heard Norah talk about it often, but I haven't actually been up here in the entire time I've lived in Mississippi. It's a lovely town. An inter-esting blend of old and new."

"It used to be more old, but over the last decade or two, they've built tons of these fancy condos for people who want game houses." They'd passed at least a dozen on their walk up Van Buren Avenue.

"Game houses?"

Reed shrugged. "Some people have weekend cabins. A lot of Ole Miss alums want a permanent base for weekend football. SEC football is serious business down here."

"Takes all kinds, I guess. I'd rather spend my weekends at the beach."

He wondered if her family had a beach house. Hell, with that kind of money, they probably had more than one. *Maybe they own a beach.* But he didn't ask. Instead, he gave himself over to telling her about Oxford, showing her the quirks and landmarks that hadn't changed on the way to the Square.

By the time they arrived for the reading, the place was pretty packed. People mingled in clusters all through the store, sipping at wine and eating canapés. Several rows of folding chairs were set up facing a podium at the back of the store. Reed paused to inhale the heady scent of old books from the locked wire cages around the shelves of first editions and rare books lining the entry wall. Beside him, Cecily clapped her hands once and bounced like a kid in a candy store, her eyes taking on the avaricious gleam of the book lover in paradise. It was sexy as hell.

"Go ahead and look around," he invited.

With a flashing grin, she began to browse. She had five titles tucked in one arm in almost as many minutes—a wide array from folklore to poetry to gardening. As she was flipping through the Greg Iles books available for purchase, the current bookstore cat leaped up on the table and demanded her attention.

"Well aren't you a beautiful thing?" She set the books aside and reached for the cat, who climbed quite willingly into her arms, then seemed content to lie there like a queen on a litter, her gray fur blending with the gray of Cecily's sweater.

"Clearly you stroked her ego in exactly the right way," he said.

Cecily rubbed her cheek against the cat's head. "She just has discerning taste. Don't you, gorgeous?"

The cat began to purr. Reed suspected he would too, if Cecily petted him.

"You should totally get a bookstore cat," she told him.

"I'd need to make sure Brenda's not allergic." He trailed off before voicing the suggestion that Cecily ought to come to the shelter with him to help pick one out.

Across the room, he saw a flash of blonde hair. It was just blonde hair. Every other woman in town had blonde hair by God or by design. But there was something in the tilt of her head that pulled at him, made him watch until she turned and he could see her face.

Reed went rigid.

No, no, no. Not here. Not now. Not while he was with Cecily. But will alone couldn't hold back the sudden wash of old resentments, shame, and defensiveness that went along with Annelise Arrington Stanton. He hadn't seen her since she'd dumped him, and he'd been fool enough to think he never would again. But he knew perfectly well that Mississippi was one big small town.

Cecily laid a hand on his arm. "Reed?" She followed his gaze to Annelise and frowned.

"Ladies and gentlemen, if you'll please take your seats."

"C'mon. Let's sit," he said.

Introductions were made and the author took his place behind the podium, greeting the crowd, making a bit of small talk before getting started. The audience sat hushed and on the edge of their seats, listening as Mississippi author Greg Iles read from his latest book. Reed didn't hear a word.

Why the hell couldn't he shake this?

Cecily's fingers laced with his and squeezed. He met her clear gray eyes. The roaring in his head stopped and the band around his chest loosened. Her mouth kicked into a half smile, her expression asking, *Okay?* Reed laid his free hand over hers and held on the rest of the reading.

As everyone rose around them to queue up

for autographs, Cecily leaned over. "Do you want to stick around or shall we try to beat the crowd to dinner?"

She was giving him an out. But that would be giving Annelise too much importance.

"Let's stick. You still have that pile of books to buy, and you wanted to get one signed. Plus, I should introduce myself as a bookseller." Reed pressed a hand to the small of her back, steering her toward the line that snaked back from the signing table.

"Reed?"

For just a moment, he froze, hand flexing against Cecily's back. Time to face the inevitable.

"Reed! It's so good to see you!"

As he turned toward his ex-girlfriend, he hoped he managed to fix his expression in something more polite than a grimace. "Annelise."

She looked a little more polished than she had in college, a little more mature. Her blonde hair was swept up in one of those careless looking updos that he knew perfectly well took her an hour to achieve. Pretentious Playboy was with her, looking self-assured and generally bored with the proceedings. Annelise's smile had a shark-like quality as she crossed over.

Had she been like that in college?

Cecily neatly stepped into Reed's side, sliding one arm around his waist, and Annelise's smile faltered just a little. Reed could've kissed her right then and there. Instead, he wrapped a comfortable arm around Cecily's shoulders and offered a more genuine smile.

"Fancy meeting you here."

"Nick and I came up for the game." Annelise tucked her arm through her husband's. "Reed, this is my husband Nick Stanton. Nick, this is Reed Campbell. He works at a little bookstore down in Wishful." She shot a glance in his direction. "Or are you doing something else now?"

Reed fought the urge to grind his teeth as he shook the other man's hand with rather more force than absolutely necessary. "I own the bookstore, actually."

"Good for you." If Annelise had any more faux sweetness in her tone, they could all drown in honey.

And he'd thought he wanted to marry this woman? Christ. Who knew she'd saved him from a fate worse than death.

Reed looked down at Cecily, "Honey, this is—"

"Oh, you must be Annelise." Cecily beamed and extended her left hand toward his ex. "Reed's told me so much about you." Reed couldn't put his finger on what it was, but something in Cecily's manner had shifted subtly, become more...regal, somehow. And suddenly he was looking at the heiress she actually was.

Annelise hesitated, eyes clearly drawn to the big honking ring glittering in the overhead lights. Where the hell had that come from? Seeming to collect herself, she shook Cecily's hand.

"I'm just so pleased to meet you. And you, Nick." Cecily shook his hand, too, before returning to a proprietary hold on Reed's arm. "Stanton. You wouldn't happen to be related to the Kenilworth Stantons, would you? I mean, not that I know them *well* since they're based in Chicago, and my family's in Greenwich, but they're just down the road from our summer house in the Hamptons." She tipped her face up to his, and Reed saw her eyes sparkle. "Remember, sweetie. It was that cute little place without a gatehouse?" Her tone was as sweet and polite as could be, while still very clearly conveying how vastly below her experience this alleged house was.

"I, uh, don't believe so," Nick said. "And you are?"

"Oh, silly me. Where are my manners?" She leveled the pair of them with a superior smile that made the cat look like an amateur. "I'm Cecily Davenport Dixon."

CHAPTER 6

"Ooohoo," REED CROWED, "THE look on her face! That was absolutely *priceless.*" As they strolled back toward the car to drop off her purchases, he gave her shoulders another squeeze. "The ring was an especially nice touch. Where'd that come from, anyway?"

"It was my grandmother's. I inherited it when she passed." Cecily shifted the antique diamond and ruby ring back to her right hand.

Reed blew a kiss toward the sky. "Thank you, Grandma, for your participation in tonight's caper. Man, Norah told me you'd done some acting, but I had no idea you were that good."

Cecily bit the inside of her lip. He thought she'd made it all up. *Damn. This is going to be harder than I thought.* "Reed, it wasn't an act."

"What are you talking about? Of course it was an act. And it was brilliantly executed. I don't think she'd have been any more impressed if you'd been the Queen Mother."

She stopped walking, towing him to a stop so that he turned to face her. "Reed, I wasn't kidding. I *am* Cecily Davenport Dixon." She waited for him to lose the smile, close off, and demand an explanation.

Instead, he brushed the hair back from her face, the humor in his expression shifting to something gentler. "I already knew you're Cecil Davenport's granddaughter. But that privileged princess back there isn't who you are. Not by a long shot."

Something warm and bright slid through

her at the acknowledgment. Then she blinked. "You *knew?* Since when?"

"The *M & S* article."

"Damn it. I thought we'd got all the copies."

Amusement shone in his hazel eyes. "I ordered more."

"Why didn't you say anything?"

"I figured you'd gone to a helluva lot of trouble to keep the secret and wouldn't appreciate that you'd been found out. Plus, we weren't exactly on close, chatty terms after I stuck my foot in it at the lake."

She opened her mouth, then closed it again, not knowing what to say.

"To be clear," he continued, "whatever invective I may have spewed about the wealthy that night was entirely specific to Annelise, whether it sounded like a generalized opinion or not."

Cecily sighed and started walking again. "I don't blame you for that opinion. God knows, I've been surrounded by that particular brand of snob most of my life. I despise it, but I know how to play the game when necessary." It was how she'd gotten into acting in the first place back in high school.

"I appreciate that you thought me worth the effort."

"She hurt you. And tonight, she was determined to resurrect that." Cecily hadn't been able to resist the urge to put Annelise in her place.

"I don't know why she bothered. She made it absolutely clear years ago that I was beneath her." He unlocked the car.

"The bigger question is what the hell you saw in her in the first place." *Hello Pot, my name is Kettle.* Cecily tossed her bag in the back seat and shut the door. "You couldn't have had anything in common, and I would've thought you weren't the kind of guy who'd fall for beauty without substance."

"She isn't without substance. She was actually on academic scholarship. But somewhere in the last semester of college, as graduation and the real world got closer, she changed her mind about what she wanted. And thank God for it. We'd have been miserable together. I can admit that now that I'm older and wiser, and in far better company." He laced his fingers with hers.

"Nice to know you learn from your mistakes." She glanced up at him, feeling suddenly shy. "I can admit I learn from mine, too. I'm sorry I didn't tell you sooner. If I'd just come right out and mentioned my family at the lake, instead of assuming you wouldn't accept it…" Where would they be if they hadn't lost the last three months?

Reed stroked his thumb along the back of her hand. "Doesn't matter. We're here now. So how about we head back to Ajax and you tell me about why you're keeping your identity a secret, while I introduce you to some of Oxford's best down home Southern cookin'?"

"Deal."

Given the crowds, Ajax Diner was popular. It took a while, but they finally got seated in one of the booths along the right wall. Local art hung over each table, and the ceiling was dotted with thousands of sandwich toothpicks that Reed told her had been shot up with drinking straws. Scents of butter and bacon and spice hung heavy in the air, making Cecily's mouth water and her empty stomach rumble. Thankfully, the dull roar of conversation kept anyone from hearing.

After they put in their orders—country fried steak for Reed and a veggie plate for her—Reed leaned forward, elbows on the table. "So, tell me your origin story, Cecily The Great."

She laughed. "I could get used to that."

"It suits you."

Cecily wasn't sure about that. She took a sip of her iced tea. "I suppose it's time for a bit of a family history lesson on the side that *isn't* constantly in the news. My dad doesn't come from the same world as my mother. He's fourth generation of a fishing family from Long Island. And when his dad had a heart attack his senior year of high school and couldn't work, my dad took the floundering fishing business and turned it into a charter company. Grandpa

Eddie was *pissed.* Said he was throwing away generations of tradition and history. But sticking to the old ways had done nothing but get them up to their eyeballs in debt, to the point that they were on the verge of losing the business by the time Dad got his hands on it. Anyway, despite a lot of resistance from the family and quite a few of the employees, he made it work, made it profitable. Grandpa Cecil hired him one summer, to sail from Long Island down to the Caribbean and back—except instead of hiring dad's boat, he hired him as captain because Dad had earned the reputation of being able to sail anything. That's how he met my mom. They deluded themselves into believing they were managing a clandestine romance on board an 82' yacht beneath the noses of her parents, both her brothers, and the other crew."

Reed's eyes twinkled in appreciation of a good story. "I gather that wasn't the case?"

"Definitely not."

"Did your grandparents object?"

"Quite the contrary. Grandpa Cecil was really impressed with what Dad had made of his company. And there was apparently a betting pool on which port they'd end up eloping in. Gran would've won, but Dad decided to be old-fashioned and asked Grandpa for Mom's hand. So they got married in a beach wedding when they got back to The Hamptons. It was quite the scandal, them being engaged after nine weeks, married in thirteen."

"Wow, that's fast."

She shrugged. "When you know, you know. I've always been kind of jealous of that. The society set assumed Mom was pregnant. Everybody who hadn't spent the summer watching them together gave the whole thing six months, a year, tops, before everything blew up. That was thirty years ago."

Cecily sat back, sipping more tea as their waitress returned with the food. "This looks amazing." She forked up a bite of the squash casserole Norah so prized and moaned in pleasure. "Okay, I concede. It's as good as Norah said it would be."

"So how did little Cecily fare as the child of two worlds?"

"We'll fast forward through the childhood and teenage years for now and just say that I grew up a happy kid, with a great family that gave me a unique perspective on people, and parents who believe in the value of hard work."

"Clearly that was a lesson you took to heart. I haven't known many people with your work ethic."

Cecily shrugged. "If you have a skill or a gift, you use it. No one on either side of my family just sits around on their laurels."

"That's consistent with everything I remember hearing about them over the years. But none of that explains why you're so intent on hiding it. You're not ashamed of them. I can hear how much you love them in the tone of your voice."

"You're right. I adore my family. But the Davenport name comes with a lot of public expectation, some merited, some not. I did my undergrad at Brown. My grandmother was an alumna there, so everybody knew who I was. And I lost track of how many people befriended or tried to date me in an attempt to access to the family fortune or reputation or political clout. I learned fast that people were a lot more interested in how they could use me and my connections than in actually developing a relationship with me."

Reed frowned. "I'm sensing a very painful life lesson here."

He'd shared his disastrous ex story with her. Time for a little quid pro quo. "Jefferson was a master's student in Public Policy."

Reed made a face. "Jefferson?"

"Jefferson Carlyle Petrie, III. And yes, he's every bit like he sounds. Old money New England, with history that can be traced back to the Mayflower."

"And you dated this guy?"

"You aren't the only one with questionable taste in significant others in college. We met spring semester my sophomore year. He was on a committee with me for a big charity fundraiser. He was charming, cultured, erudite, and he put all of his considerable skill into wooing me. I fell hard and fast." She'd gotten past beating herself up for that. Mostly.

"We were really well-suited. He was charitably-minded, as I am. Interested in improving things from a policy and systemic level."

"Meaning he was politically-minded," Reed concluded.

"Yes. And because of my background, I'd been groomed to be the perfect political partner. We had big dreams about how we'd change the world." Cecily still ached a little at the loss of those dreams.

"We started by founding a charity for disabled veterans, bridging the gap between what the VA provides and what's actually needed. Physical therapy, better prosthetics, other forms of continuing care for those not located near a VA hospital. I funded the start up and set up the initial marketing push to bring in additional donations, but I was still in school, so I left a lot of the running of it to the board, which really meant Jefferson, since he was the chair. He was running for state representative at the time, and the public just ate it up that he was taking time out from the political trail to take care of disabled veterans. The fact that he was linked with me and my family just added further legitimacy to his campaign."

"I feel like this is heading toward a very predictable, very messy end."

"I didn't predict it. I didn't have a friggin' clue." Her hand fisted around the fork at the memory. She forced it to relax. "A reporter from the *Providence Journal* asked for a meeting with me about The Hero's Help Alliance. Since I did a lot of the marketing, that wasn't an unusual thing. But when I showed up for the meeting, I faced a roomful of people who'd applied for the program. Despite the fact that they'd all been approved, they'd seen nothing.

"The reporter could've raked me over the coals, dragged my reputation through the muck, but he'd done his homework about my family and thought it highly unlikely I knew anything untoward was going on. So, he helped me set up a sting instead. And we found out that Jefferson had embezzled over eighty percent of the charity's funds, funneling it into his political campaign, and tying up the rest in a messy financial knot that made it hard to immediately track."

They'd also found out that, in typical politician fashion, he'd had a woman on the side. But that wasn't germane to this discussion.

"Please tell me he's rotting in a cell."

"Oh no. Old money, remember. Top notch lawyers. But my family made certain that any future political aspirations he may have will be dead in the water. And then we made good on all the applicants who'd been shafted by Jefferson's embezzlement. After which, we elected an entirely new board, established oversight by some other people my family trusts, and I stepped out of the charity entirely."

"Stepped out willingly or were forced out?"

Oh, he was far too good at reading between the lines.

"I was strongly encouraged to step out, with the irrefutable logic that I wouldn't be able to oversee anything while I was in graduate school."

"That must've been really hard on you. Walking away from what you'd created. Something you felt that strongly about."

She'd hated it. Hated feeling like she'd failed her family and insulted their legacy. They'd never said a word about it, but they hadn't had to. The rest of the media hadn't been as understanding as that initial reporter from the *Providence Journal.* Most of the coverage had focused on Jefferson, but there'd been plenty of speculation about her. Dropping out of the public eye had been the only way to survive.

Cecily jerked her shoulder in a shrug. "It was an expensive lesson not to be foolish in who I trust. So when I left for Northwestern, I left the Davenport name behind, along with the money and status that went with it."

"Did they cut you off?"

"I cut myself off, other than making the occasional charitable donation. I decided that whatever I did from then on, whatever I achieved, would be on my own merit. I'd sink or swim on my own and it wouldn't reflect on them. And it ended up being this incredibly freeing thing, to be judged on who *I* am, not on who my family is. It's just been my standard operating procedure ever since."

"So, nobody you've dated since college has known what you come from?"

She set the fork down and wet her throat with the last of the tea before answering. "Nobody's mattered enough to bring it up until now."

REED EYED CECILY'S dark house as he pulled into the drive. "Think Christoff is asleep?"

"He's either over at Daniel's or he's lying in wait to pounce on me for details the moment I walk through the door." She shot an amused glance his way. "He was always on your side."

"Good to know." Reed got out and hurried around to open her door. "Ma'am."

She took his offered hand. "You Southern boys certainly have pretty manners."

"Some old-fashioned things are worth retaining." He kept her hand in his as they walked up to the front porch, not wanting the night to end.

"You want to sit for a little while?"

He smiled, glad they were on the same page. "Sure."

She led him over to the little glider.

Reed took the seat beside her and ran his hand over the wooden arm of the glider. "I've never seen one quite like this."

"It's made of upcycled shipping pallets."

"Seriously?"

"Daniel made it. You should see some of the things he can put together. He's working on starting a business of it. The Pallet Palace. I did his website back in the summer. Right now, it's largely custom orders, since he doesn't have a place to store stock, but he hopes to expand eventually." She tugged a blanket off the back. "It's a bit chilly tonight."

"Welcome to fall in Mississippi. Summer temps in the daytime and cold at night. C'mon." Reed opened his arms in invitation.

She tucked the blanket around their legs and snuggled in close, resting her head against his chest. He decided it was an almost perfect end to a pretty perfect night—run-in with Annelise notwithstanding.

"Did you get what you needed out of the reading?"

Cecily laughed. "Was that really why you asked me to go?"

"Partly. Mostly I wanted to see you in my world. You fit pretty well. For a Yankee."

"Really? That's the part you focus on after everything you know about me?"

So sure she'd be judged on her affluent background. He skimmed his fingers through her silky hair, resisting the urge to bury his nose in the sweet, lemony scent. "It's the only relevant part. You passed the cornbread test."

"It *was* damned good cornbread." On a contented sigh, she said, "I had fun."

"Good. There's a lot of other stuff I want to show you to further your southern education."

"Oh yeah? Like what?"

"The Sweet Potato Festival is only a few weeks off."

"Sweet potatoes?" Her voice dripped with skepticism.

"Sure. Vardaman is the sweet potato capital of the world. Once you've had sweet potato pie, you'll never go back to pumpkin."

"Blasphemer! There is no Thanksgiving without pumpkin pie."

"I'll concede that it's worth having both."

"Generous of you."

"I'm pretty sure there's no such thing as too much pie."

She grinned up at him. "I've eaten your grandmother's pie. This is a true thing. What else?"

"Well, there's the Spring pilgrimage in Columbus. It's not as grand as the one in Natchez, but it's closer and easier to manage. You'll totally dig all the folks that dress up in period clothes to give the tours of all the antebellum homes."

Reed knew as soon as the words left his mouth that it was the wrong thing to say. He could actually see the reality of their situation come crashing back down on her. Every fiber of his being wanted to rewind, have a do-over as the light in her eyes dimmed and her expression twisted into regret.

"Reed—"

Please don't say it.

She pulled away from him, tugging the blanket up to her chin. "I don't know how much longer I'm here."

"Have you signed a contract somewhere?"

"No, but I have to be ready to go when I do. I could be moving in a matter of weeks. Probably will be. I've got resumes out at all the top tier firms on my short list. These are prestigious positions, so there's a big possibility I won't get offered a job."

"But if you do get an offer, you're gone." Reed saw past her false modesty. She was amazing at what she did. If any of these places interviewed her, that would be the end of it.

She gave a *What can I do?* shrug.

There was plenty she could do. With the means at her disposal, she could stay if she really wanted to. But he knew how much she wanted to succeed on her own terms, without the help of her family, so he didn't say a word. How could he, when he admired the hell out of her choice to do exactly that? He'd known her leaving was a very real possibility when he decided to pursue her again. But he'd thought he'd have more time to convince her that staying here was the right move. As usual he'd miscalculated.

He sighed. "I know how hard you've worked for this." Sometimes it was a real pisser to be able to see both sides of a situation.

"I like you, Reed. I've always liked you. But I

just don't think it's smart to start something when I might not be around to finish it."

"So, what exactly was tonight then?"

"I don't know. Part business. Part apology. Part what if?"

He nodded, though he didn't know what he was agreeing with. His mind was full of his own what ifs. What if he hadn't said the wrong thing at the lake? What if they'd had the last three months to deepen the connection between them? Would she still be planning to leave?

They were useless questions. He had; they hadn't; and she was. That was reality.

At least she hadn't called it a mistake.

Looking over at her, he hated the mix of concern and sorrow on her face. "You aren't going to start avoiding me again, are you?"

Even in the moonlight, he could see her blush.

"No. Quite apart from the fact that I still have a job to do, I'd like to be friends."

The whole idea left a sour taste in his

mouth. But it wasn't like he wanted to hurt her by saying no.

"Sure." He rose, letting the blanket slide off his lap. "It's late. I should be getting on home."

Cecily unfolded and dug out her key. "See you on Monday?"

"Yeah. You know where to find me." Reed waited until she'd unlocked the door, then took a step back, lifting a hand in a completely lame wave before shoving both hands in his pockets to keep from reaching for her. "Night."

He could feel Cecily's gaze on him as he walked to his car and wondered what she was thinking. Was she second guessing her decision? No, that was probably wishful thinking.

One foot in front of the other. Do not open your mouth and embarrass yourself any further.

His phone buzzed with an incoming text as he slid into the driver's seat. Pulling it out, he found a message from Selina.

You're quiet tonight.

Because I've been spending time with a real girl,

not a figment of technology and imagination. For all the good it's done me.

Reed: **Just watching something I want slip out of my reach.**

Selina: **So go after it. You still might not get it, but at least you'll have tried.**

A light went on in the house and Cecily shut the door. He cranked the car, staring at the phone until the screen went dark. He didn't want this. Didn't want a fake girlfriend. Didn't want the lie. He wanted the woman he'd just walked away from. And how was she to know that if he didn't man up and show her?

Reed turned off the engine and sprinted across the yard.

Cecily opened the door before he could knock. "Reed? Did you forget something?"

"Yeah." He stepped inside, spearing his hands into her hair and claiming her mouth before she could say another word.

Her body gave one quick jolt, her hands coming up to his shoulders. Reed braced to be pushed away, maybe slapped. Then she shuddered and opened to him on a sexy little moan, moving in and wrapping her arms around his neck. Reed kicked the door shut and backed her up against it, caging her with his body, while he devoured her mouth. This wasn't the slow, languid exploration at the lake. It was pure, unadulterated wanting. He had just enough control to keep his hands in her hair, rather than sprinting over the body she pressed against his.

When he felt even that thread begin to fray, he gentled the kiss and forced himself to ease back, pressing his brow to hers as his breath heaved, fast and unsteady. "I don't wanna be friends. I'd rather have this time with you now and be torn up when you go than have nothing at all."

"Sweetie, if you don't say yes to him after that display, I'm checking you into the nearest mental hospital."

Reed cranked his head around to see Christoff smirking with approval from the hall.

Well, too late for embarrassment. "That'd be Whitfield. Just so you know."

"Noted," he said cheerfully.

Cecily tipped Reed's face back toward hers, rubbing a thumb along the scruff of his jaw. "Not necessary. I may be crazy, but it won't be for saying no. Now, go away, Christoff," she said, and tugged Reed's mouth down to hers.

CHAPTER 7

"THANK YOU SO MUCH for having me." Cecily had on her best Sunday company smile, but nerves jittered underneath as she stepped into Grammy Campbell's house, Reed on her heels.

"Of course, sugar. You come right on in. Oh here, let me take those." Grammy tugged the covered basket from Cecily's hands before she could protest. "Everybody's in the living room. Anita brought cookies to tide everybody over until dinner's ready."

Reed brightened. "Snickerdoodles?"

"What else would I make my favorite son?" his mother said, coming into the foyer and pulling him into a hug.

Was that supposed to be some kind of warning?

"I'm your only son," Reed pointed out.

She lifted both brows. "Do you want me to take the cookies back?"

"No ma'am," he said solemnly.

Cecily stood to one side, her hands clasped in a death grip since she no longer had the basket of biscuits to keep them occupied. Reed reached over to tangle her fingers with his, giving her a squeeze that was, no doubt, meant to be comforting.

His mother beamed. "Cecily, it's good to see you again."

"Thank you, Mrs. Campbell." God, was that stiff and formal tone really coming out of her mouth?

"Oh no, there are far too many of those in this house. Anita. Y'all go ahead and get some cookies. I'll just be helping Mama in the kitchen."

Reed bent to Cecily's ear. "Relax. You know everybody here. They already like you."

"I wasn't dating you before," she murmured.

"Even better. Then you know they like *you* and aren't just pretending because you're attached to me."

Oh, like that helped anything?

They stepped into the living room. "Hey, hey, the gang's all here!" Reed exchanged fist bumps with his cousins Mitch and Cam, hugs with his other cousin, Miranda, and his Aunt Liz and Aunt Sandy, and a firm handshake with his Uncle Pete. Cecily was proud she actually remembered who all of them were. She gave her own greetings and made a beeline for Norah.

Reed went to the sideboard to pour them both drinks. "Where's Dad?"

"Manning the grill," Mitch replied. "His turn on rotation."

"Who's got the fire extinguisher?" Reed

asked, offering Cecily a glass. "Here. This will help."

Cecily shot him a look of gratitude as she accepted the wine and took a hefty swallow.

"I heard that. I'll have you know I haven't burned anything in a month," Jimmy protested, coming back inside, a pair of tongs still in his hand.

Uncle Pete grinned. "We have backup timers set."

Reed mimed wiping his brow. "Oh good. Then we'll all still get to eat."

Norah intervened before the teasing escalated into an argument. "Well, now that you're here and adequately armed, I call for a celebratory toast. The Madrigal Theater is officially back on track." She lifted her wine glass and clinked it with Cecily's.

"Here's to that. How was the party?" Cecily leaned back against the arm of the sofa, crossing her feet and wishing her bitch boots made her feel more confident.

"It was great. And really more of a gossipfest. Tyler and Brody were supposed to be the guests of honor—the structural damage to the theater couldn't have been fixed without them—but Tyler called to say they'd be late, then they didn't show at all."

"Really?" Cecily punctuated the question with a suggestive eyebrow waggle.

"Brody's truck wasn't collected from the job site until this afternoon," Cam reported.

"Dude, you're such a girl," Reed told him.

"Hey, they're two of my best friends. I have a stake in them getting back together. If it doesn't work, I have to kick his ass for breaking her heart again."

Reed snagged Cecily around the waist, pulling her into him. "What's your interest in this? You barely know Tyler, and have you even met Brody?"

She curled her fingers through his belt loops and grinned up at him, the contact doing what the alcohol had not and dissipating the nerves. "Are you kidding? Living in a small town is like being in the middle of a soap opera. I've been following the will they/won't they second chance romance of those two for weeks. *So* much better than *Days of Our Lives.*"

"Stupendously intelligent, talented, classy, and a soap opera addict?"

Cecily narrowed her eyes. "None of those things are mutually exclusive."

"Of course not. It's just unexpected and… very humanizing."

"It's all Christoff's fault. Living with him means I've developed a much higher drama quotient than I used to have."

"I don't know," Norah drawled. "He's toned down a lot since Daniel."

"He's still Christoff," Cecily insisted. "He's just…more cheerful."

"Speaking of celebratory toasts," Anita said, coming back into the living room, "Reed, I heard from Marie Lanning the other day. You remember her? She's one of my old sorority sisters. Her son Shawn and Reed were good friends back in summer camp." Anita added, clearly for Cecily's benefit. "Anyway, she and Doug are down on the coast now."

Cecily's gaze followed Reed as he grabbed up one of the cookies and bit in. "Yeah? What's Shawn up to?"

"Living in Virginia Beach. He and his wife are expecting their first baby in February."

"Good for them." He took another bite of the cookie, offered it to Cecily for a nibble.

She bit in, enjoying the sweet bite of cinnamon and sugar as it melted on her tongue. Now *that* was a snickerdoodle.

"She was wishing you congratulations, too."

"For what?"

"On your engagement."

Cecily choked as the bite of cookie slid into her windpipe.

"Seems she ran into Annelise, who said she'd run into you and your fiancée in Oxford. Is there something you two want to tell us?" Her brows quirked expectantly.

Reed ignored his mother, peering closely at Cecily. "You okay?"

She coughed a few times, waving a hand until she caught her breath. "I seriously under-estimated the whole Mississippi being one big small town factor," she wheezed.

"Been tellin' you that since you moved down here," Norah said.

"Yes, we ran into Annelise, but I never said we were engaged," Reed's lips twitched as he looked back at Cecily. "I mean, we might have implied it."

She couldn't resist smiling back. "Okay, let's be honest here. It's possible that I have an overdeveloped sense of justice, and when I met the heinous hellbeast that was his ex, I decided to put her in her place."

"By pretending you were some kind of heiress?" Anita asked.

Damn. Seemed her plan for revenge had worked even better than expected if Annelise had been running her mouth that much. Reed looked to Cecily, clearly waiting for her to tele-graph whether he needed to cover or shift the conversation. That he was deferring to her on this point gave her all the warm fuzzies. He'd keep her secret, if she wanted. But if they were going to make anything of their relationship, his family would have to be clued in eventually.

Cecily took a breath and squared her shoulders. "Actually, that part wasn't a lie. I'm Cecil Davenport's granddaughter.

Grammy gaped. "Davenport? As in the philanthropist?"

Cecily actually smiled a little at that. "He'd be pleased that's the first thing you thought of. I don't tend to mention it—ever—because people usually get weird. But it is, occasionally, useful."

"Well, I'd never have guessed," Grammy said. "You're so down-to-earth."

"Thank you. I take that as an enormous compliment."

"Mom," Reed interrupted, "what exactly did you say to Mrs. Wallace?" No doubt the last thing he wanted was for the truth to be making its way back to his ex.

"I pretended I knew exactly what she was talking about and said I was getting a wonderful daughter-in-law, even if she is a Yankee. Which is, for the record, exactly what I'd have said if you *were* engaged." Reed's mom shot a pointed look in his direction.

Cecily's cheeks heated. "I, uh, well, thank you."

"Okay, let's stop embarrassing the girl. It's time for dinner," Grammy announced.

EVERYBODY MOVED THROUGH THE KITCHEN, grabbing bowls and platters on their way to the dining room. Cecily placed a basket full of steaming biscuits on the corner of the table and sat down. "Contributed by Beth, of the soon-to-open Dixieland Biscuit Company."

Norah started the passing of the food. "The launch plan you laid out is fabulous."

"It was a lot of fun. I mean, how often did we get to make people happy with what we did at Helios?" she asked, referring to the firm she and Norah had worked for in Chicago. "Biscuits make people happy."

Reed bit into one and moaned as the fluffy, buttery goodness hit his tongue. "Yes. Yes, they do," he said.

Clearly the work made *her* happy. She fairly glowed as she told Norah about the rest of what she'd lined up. Reed had never seen her get that spark when she talked about the other prospective jobs she was applying for. Not that she talked about them at all, if she could help it. They'd spent the last two weeks powering full-steam ahead, spending every spare minute together in case those minutes were numbered. He even managed to forget, for a few hours at a time, that they might be.

"Does she need help with anything?" Norah asked.

"No. She's down to finalizing delivery of the backer prizes and getting the first printing of Biscuit Company t-shirts. Then it should be good to go for the grand opening."

"You ever gonna tell Beth?"

Cecily forked up some potatoes. "Nope."

"Tell her what?" Reed asked.

Norah arched a questioning brow at Cecily and everything clicked.

"You were the mystery backer," he said. Everybody in town had been speculating for weeks, but they'd generally assumed it'd been Gerald Peyton, CEO of the non-profit Norah was working with on a number of restoration projects around town.

"I was." Cecily said it with the same faintly embarrassed tone she might've admitted, "I was the secret admirer."

Reed tried to wrap his brain around that. She'd told him that she didn't touch the family fortunes except for charity. He didn't know what he'd imagined that meant, but dropping five grand as casually as fifty bucks wasn't it.

"How often do you do this kind of thing?" Aunt Liz asked.

Cecily shrugged. "It's not like it's a regular, scheduled thing. Just depends on what presents itself and when. And whether I can do it anonymously. Everyone in my family has pet causes and organizations. But I've always been drawn more to the personal. I like seeing the impact, knowing that the money went where it was supposed to go and gets a reasonably immediate return on my investment. It's a rush."

"Why anonymous?" Cam asked.

Reed gave him a pitying look. "No self-respecting superhero wants actual credit."

Cecily's lips quirked. "And what do self-respecting superheroes want?"

"They're all in it for different reasons, usually relating to some inner wound. Oliver Queen is driven to right the wrongs of his father and save his city from corruption. Spiderman has to overcome the regret of not saving Uncle Ben, and be the kind of man Uncle Ben would have been proud of. Batman has to clean up Gotham so no other kids have to grow up without their parents."

Intrigue mixed with amusement. "And me?"

"In your case, with great privilege comes great responsibility. To paraphrase Uncle Ben.

You're too driven to prove yourself—and earn things on your own merit—to be comfortable with the fact that you were born to affluence. But you have it, so you feel compelled to use it to help those who need it—particularly those who may be overlooked by others or who wouldn't be helped by more conventional means. Recognition of your good deeds would minimize them because then people would be focused on you instead of the person or cause you supported, so you prefer to stay in the metaphoric shadows."

Her look of flirty amusement slid away, leaving an uncharacteristic vulnerability in its wake as she stared at him. "Is that really how you see me?"

"Am I wrong?" he asked quietly.

"No, that's…stunningly accurate." And she looked absolutely flummoxed by it.

"Who knew your addiction to comic books would make you an armchair psychologist," Cam said, in an obvious effort to lighten the mood.

"Any good student of literature is an armchair psychologist," Reed retorted. "Literature is all about exploration of human nature. Just because my choice of literature happens to involve a lot of spandex, capes, and ass kicking doesn't make that any less true."

Cecily's phone began to ring. "Sorry," she muttered. She slipped it out of her pocket and started to send it to voicemail, then hesitated as she read the display. "Excuse me, I need to take this." Pushing back from the table, she strode out of the room.

"That's quite the woman you've got there, son," Jimmy said.

"Yeah, she's pretty damned amazing." And Reed could only thank God—and Norah—that they'd finally connected.

"Gotta say, I'm pretty proud of the Campbell men right now," Aunt Sandy said. "Mitch, you're falling behind here."

"Hey, leave my love life out of this," Mitch protested.

"Your lack of love life, you mean," Miranda said.

"Oh you're one to talk," he shot back.

As the sniping continued around the table, Reed just smiled. Until he saw Cecily walk back in, face pale.

He was already half out of his chair, his napkin tossed to the table. "What's wrong?"

But she wasn't looking at him as the room fell silent. She was looking at Norah. "You could've warned me. When did they call?"

Norah grimaced. "Friday. I didn't think they'd call you until tomorrow, and I wanted you to have the weekend not to have to think about it."

"Excuse me, think about what?" Reed asked.

But he knew. Even before Cecily turned stricken eyes on him. "I have an interview with Verdant."

That meant exactly nothing to Reed. He just shook his head, looking for some kind of elucidation.

"They're one of the top ten marketing firms in the country," Norah said quietly.

Of course they were. Because a Davenport wouldn't settle for anything less. "Where?" Reed asked

Cecily inhaled a shaky breath. "San Francisco."

With those two words, the axe that had been hovering over the back of his neck for weeks finally fell.

"I'm sorry," she whispered, misery etched in every line of her face.

What was he supposed to say to that? Manners asserted themselves in the absence of a rational response. He straightened fully. "Congratulations."

Cecily flinched as if he'd slapped her. "I… excuse me, I need a minute."

For several humming beats, silence reigned. Reed didn't know what to do. Should he go after her? Give her a few minutes to compose herself?

Mitch was the one who broke it. "Okay,

does anybody else feel like we've already done this?"

"She's not me," Norah cautioned. "The circumstances aren't the same."

No, they weren't the same. But they were close enough that Reed had been planning for this. "Did you get the stuff I asked you for?"

"In my purse. It's not as complete as I'd like but given the time constraints..."

Reed nodded. "Thanks."

He'd foolishly believed he'd have more time to lay the groundwork. Slow and methodical was his way. But the clock had run out. He had to trust that she felt this connection between them, too. That she'd be willing to take a risk on it. On them.

"What are you going to do?" his mother asked.

"Take a leap."

CHAPTER 8

ECILY WISHED SHE HADN'T answered. It would only have delayed the inevitable, but at least the night wouldn't have been ruined. She hadn't been able to lie when she'd come back to the table—wouldn't have insulted Reed by trying. And it was obvious from the look on his face that he already knew. So they both suffered through the rest of what became the world's most awkward dinner, with everybody looking worried and biting back whatever opinions they had on the subject.

As they drove back toward town, Reed took her hand without a word.

He made her want to be reckless. To just rush in, without thought to consequences or cost. And, to a point, for the last couple of weeks, she had rushed in, ignoring the countdown in the back of her brain, because while she was with him, it didn't matter. Nothing else mattered. She looked at him and saw the possibility of what Norah had with Cam, and she wanted that. She'd be insane not to want it. But a part of her kept hesitating. She didn't trust her judgment well enough to know if she was projecting, or if what was between them was really real. So she'd held a piece of herself back, and now the final countdown had begun and circumstances would force a decision, one way or the other. After everything she'd worked for, how could she make that call, how could she know for sure that reckless plunge would be worth it, based on a matter of mere weeks?

And yet...he saw *her.* Not the money. Not the pedigree. Not the act. Her. She'd misjudged him so badly. How could she sit beside this amazing, astute man, and not feel physically ill at being poised to walk away?

"I hate this," she burst out.

"I know."

"You're not going to try to talk me out of it?"

Reed glanced at her. "You know I want you to stay. My trying to guilt you into it would make me a selfish bastard and wouldn't be a good foundation for any future relationship. Besides, you feel bad enough already."

That was true enough. But it wouldn't have stopped a lot of men.

"So no, no guilt trip. I've got something else in mind."

"You do?" Her heart gave a hopeful leap. As he bypassed the turn for her street, she sat up a little straighter. "Where are we going?"

"Downtown. I thought we'd take a little walk. I think better when I'm moving."

He parked at the far end of the green. Cecily slid out of his SUV and hunched into her coat at a sudden gust of wind, thinking that a single summer below the Mason-Dixon line had made her soft if she felt a chill in the low fifties. But, as the breeze ruffled her hair, she felt the first bite of true autumn on the air. Reed circled around and tucked her arm through his.

"Did you know Norah nearly walked away from Cam?"

Surprise had her step faltering. "What? Why?"

"Because she thought picking him would mean giving up her career. She is, as you well know, incredibly driven—you're a lot alike in that respect. Cam's more like me. Very rooted to life here. She couldn't see how they could make it work and, frankly, neither could we."

"We?" she asked.

"You've met my family. We were all up in the middle of that."

She had no trouble whatsoever imagining it.

"I'm ashamed to say we didn't exactly react positively when we found out the two of them were involved. Not because we didn't love Norah—because we always have—but just because we worried it wouldn't work, and we didn't want to see either of them hurt. Which she absolutely knew. She gave a speech."

Cecily laughed. "Of course she did."

"It helped. We could see how much she cared for him. And we could also see how it was absolutely tearing her up, feeling like she had to choose." He pulled her to a stop beside the fountain at the heart of town, taking both her hands in his. "You've got that same look."

"I don't have as many years of career invested as she did when Helios fired her, but yeah, I absolutely feel that. I've worked really hard to do what I've done, trying to live up to my family's expectations and the burden of the family legacy. I don't want to throw that away." She squeezed his hands. "But I don't want to throw this away either."

"Do you think staying would be throwing it all away because you can't see yourself living a small-town life long-term or because you don't see how what you do is applicable here?" She opened her mouth to speak but he continued.

"And I don't ask that because I think you think less of small-town living. I know you don't."

She answered without hesitation. "If there was a job—a *real* job, with real potential and opportunities here—we wouldn't be having this conversation."

Some of the tension left him, and Cecily realized how rigidly controlled he'd been since dinner.

"Okay then." He dug in his pocket and placed a quarter in her palm. "Make your wish."

The metal was still warm from his body heat. Cecily looked at it, then back up at him. "Seriously?"

"You can't live in a place like Wishful and not believe in the lore."

When Norah had told her that the fountain was fed by nearby Hope Springs and had been granting wishes in one form or another since it was built just after the Civil War, Cecily had assumed it was just an adorable marketing spin on the town's quirky name. But she'd learned that the locals, at least, believed. Did she?

"Why's it my wish instead of yours?"

"I'm not the one at a crossroads."

Cecily cupped the coin in her palm. If she wished for an answer, what would the fountain tell her? She wasn't sure she *really* bought into the idea of wishes as anything more than a romantic notion, but Wishful was touted as the town where hope sprang eternal and she could sure as hell use some of that, so she figured it was worth a shot.

Which path am I meant to choose? She tossed the coin into the water. Not exactly the classic *I wish* formula, but none of the stories she'd heard since coming to Wishful specified that you had to ask a certain way.

They both watched until the ripples faded and the glint of treasure shone beneath the water's surface.

"Now what?" she asked.

"Now we walk a little more."

Reed obviously had something in mind so she linked her arm through his again, snuggling close for warmth, and followed his lead.

As they left the green, headed down Spring Street, he began again. "So I've already told you that my family was all up in the middle of Cam and Norah. We aren't exactly known for our subtlety as a group. We all felt awful that Norah thought she had to defend her relationship with Cam, so since she couldn't figure out how she could stay, we took it upon ourselves to come up with a plan."

"Something other than her becoming the new City Planner?"

"Yeah, that wasn't even on the table at that point. We were focused on proving that there was, in fact, a need for her services in a town of this size. So we utilized the groundwork and rapport she'd already built by starting the citizen's coalition and reviving the Chamber of Commerce to secure letters of intent from almost every business in town, expressing interest in marketing services, should she decide to open her own firm. Uncle Pete pulled together all the paperwork necessary to file for a business license. Mitch drew up plans to renovate this place into her dream office." Reed stopped in front of the old train station. "And we ran over her like a stampede of elephants."

"How did she take that?"

"Oh, she was gracious about it—she's Norah, after all—and once she got over feeling backed into a corner, she really got into the idea. It'd never even crossed her mind to open her own firm. Obviously, this isn't what she ended up doing. But there's no reason why you couldn't take the same plan and adapt it to you."

Was he crazy? "Open my own firm? At twenty-four? With no professional reputation to speak of?"

"You have plenty of professional reputation here. You're damned good at this kind of work, and you love doing it. There's a documented need for the kind of services y'all can provide. It's part of why Norah has those two days of open consult a week, even though it's really more than she has time to deal with on top of being City Planner. And I know for a fact she's been passing a lot of it off to you. It's not the kind of corporate accounts you'd work with at Verdant, but it's a different kind of challenge. One that appeals to you, or you wouldn't have stayed here this far past the end of your internship."

"Something like this would take considerable startup capital."

"Which we both know you have, should you choose to use it." He held up his hand for silence. "I know you don't want to touch that money for yourself, but consider how many people you could help if you were properly set up. And it's not like you have to do anything on a grand scale to start. There's no rule book that says you have to have an office to accept clients right off. People like it if you come to them. Makes them feel important. And you've said yourself, you tend to get a better feel for a business when you spend some time there."

Even as excitement began to hum in her blood, she had to force herself to slow down, consider all the angles.

"There's one major problem with this scenario."

"What's that?"

"All those letters of intent are for Norah's skills. I'm not Norah. I'd never pretend to be."

"You're every bit as good as she is. Better, even, at some things."

"That's sweet, Reed, but you're not exactly an unbiased party here."

"I agree, but it's not coming from me. Norah's said so herself. Which is why she got these." He reached into his coat pocket and handed her a folded sheaf of papers.

Cecily unfolded them. "What's this?"

"Signatures from all the business owners in town who want to work with you. Not quite as comprehensive as what we pulled together before, but we were operating on a much shorter time-frame, with less manpower. I didn't figure you'd appreciate being bowled over either, so I didn't loop in the rest of the family. Still, it should be enough to prove viability of the concept."

"Norah did this for me?"

"I thought it was my idea when I took it to her, but as usual, she was five steps ahead of me. She said she owed you. If I hadn't brought it up, she would have."

A hard knot lodged in Cecily's throat as she stared at the list of names spanning more than three full sheets of paper.

She could stay.

She could do the work she loved, putting both her skills and her inheritance to good use helping people. Just like Norah, she could put her own mark on reviving this charming little town. And she could see where things went with this smart, funny, incredibly caring man, who'd gone to all this trouble to give her an option that would fit within her personal principles.

As the silence stretched out, Reed seemed to lose a little of his certainty. "You don't have to give an answer right now. I know we're not... things aren't...I wouldn't expect you to make a decision without going and doing the interview and taking time to gather all the facts. I just wanted to even the playing field and make sure you knew you had another choice."

The knot in her throat dissolved, leaving a spreading warmth in her chest. Cecily rose to her toes, sliding her arms around his neck and bringing his face close to hers. "The only choice I'm concerned with right this moment is whose house is closer—yours or mine?"

"You'll have to excuse the mess. If I'd known we were coming back here, I'd have picked up some." Reed's furtive glance around—checking for dirty laundry or who knew what—made Cecily grin.

"Unless you've been eating potato chips in bed and haven't bothered to change the sheets, I really don't care. I'm not here for the grand tour." But, as it was her first time here, she looked her fill of Reed's space.

The downtown apartment held the same

cozy comfort of Inglenook, with a leather sofa and overstuffed chair flanked on all sides by bookcases. Huge, framed comic posters marched along one wall, and assorted action figures perched along shelves. No dirty laundry or stacks of take-out containers littered the coffee table. Predictably, books were scattered on every horizontal surface, with bookmarks and sticky tabs bristling from most. She wondered how many of them he'd actually read.

"A fair chunk."

"What?" she asked.

Reed slid her coat from her shoulders. "Everybody always wants to know how many of them I've read."

"Considering it looks like you could open a second branch of Inglenook out of your living room, it's a reasonable question." There were even books lining shelves in the kitchen. Their spines made a colorful patchwork along the neutral walls.

"There's no such thing as too many books," he insisted. "Want wine?"

Wine was a delaying tactic, a chance to quiet nerves or back out. But Cecily was through hesitating. "Maybe later." She turned into him, sliding her hands up to his shoulders.

Reed's hands curved around her hips and held her where she stood, still a little apart from him. His hazel eyes searched hers. "Are you sure?"

She'd said as much by the fountain, but he wouldn't be Reed if he wasn't a gentleman to the last.

"I'm sure I want this. I want you."

His eyes flared and his hands tightened as he stepped into her. Then his mouth was on hers and she realized how much he'd banked the heat the past few weeks. He went from zero to laser focused in 2.5 seconds. The floor seemed to tip beneath her feet, and she realized he was propelling them both across the room. Digging her heels in, she laid both hands against his chest. Reed stopped, pulling back to look at her in concern.

"Better idea," she said and bounced up to wrap her legs around his waist.

"Definitely," he breathed, then took her mouth again.

Freed of the burden of balance, Cecily threaded her fingers through his hair and slanted her head to take the kiss deeper. The hardness behind his fly rubbed against her center as he walked, a delicious preview of things to come. They bumped up against something. She felt the press of a shelf against her shoulder and dropped her head back with a moan. "How did you know I had a fantasy about you and me and a bookcase?"

He chuckled against her throat. "Did you now?" His tongue skated along the length of her collar bone.

"God, yes. Ever since that day I bought Blair's birthday present."

"I'll file that away for another time," he promised. "Tonight, I want you in my bed."

Something snicked and the press of the bookcase fell away.

"What the—?" Cecily turned her head to see the bookcase opening into a passageway. "*Shut up.* Your bedroom is behind a hidden door?"

Reed laughed. "I wanted to maximize shelf space along this wall, so yeah, I installed a bookcase on the door. The hidden passage effect is a bonus."

"Definite bonus," she declared as he carried her down the short hall, past a bathroom and into the bedroom.

He tumbled them both onto the mattress, nipping at her bottom lip before rolling away. Cecily made a sound of protest.

"I want to see you," he said.

A lamp flicked on. She blinked a bit as her eyes adjusted, then noticed the faint look of horror on his face. "What is it?"

"I…um…wasn't expecting company."

Cecily looked down at the bed and saw the Batman sheets.

"They were a gag gift from Mitch. I didn't see any reason for perfectly good sheets to go to waste." His ears had gone adorably pink.

She reached out and curled her fingers around his belt, tugging him back toward her. "Somehow I don't think it's the Dark Knight who's rising at the moment." To illustrate the point, she rubbed her knuckles down the erection straining his jeans.

Reed made a strangled noise. "Vixen."

Cecily only grinned and began to work at his belt.

He shook his head and backed out of reach. "Nope. Ladies first."

He crouched down, taking hold of her boots and pulling her toward the edge of the bed. Releasing one, he ran his hands along her calf to where the zipper started. Cecily felt the burn of his touch even through the leather.

"Do you have any idea what kind of fantasies I've had about these boots?"

"The kind that will, I hope, someday combine really well with mine about the bookcase."

"Wasn't even in the top five, but now that you mention it..." His gaze ran up the length of her, and the look in his eyes had her wishing she was wearing a skirt instead of skinny jeans.

He took his time, unzipping one boot with such slow, deliberate focus she felt like he'd exposed more than her pant leg by the time he slipped it off. Why, oh why, hadn't she worn a skirt tonight? He finished with the second boot and set the pair of them neatly aside. Jesus, even the sight of him being *neat* was a turn on. Or maybe it was that now that they were here, in his room, in his bed, he didn't seem to be in any particular hurry. Like they had all night. Or forever. And because of his planning, they did.

Something shifted in Cecily's chest, a last piece of her heart cracking open as he crawled beside her on the bed. She was in love with him. She was in love with him, and he'd given her the means to stay. There was no more reason to hesitate, no more reason to hold back.

She wrapped her arms around him, pulling his lips back to hers as she poured out everything she wasn't quite ready to say. He met her heat in equal measure, hands touching, taking, working some kind of magic on buttons and zippers, until the warmth of his palm skimmed across her belly and lower, beneath the edge of her bikini briefs.

"Oh!" She'd been about to say something, but the moment his fingers cupped her sex, every thought melted right out of her head, save one. "More."

She arched into his touch, maddened by the pressure of his hand trapped against her. The jeans limited his movement, but oh, dear Lord, what he managed to do with just a little friction. She wanted the jeans off, but that required more coordination than she could manage just now and his fingers felt so damned good… Her body bowed as she shot over the first peak.

Reed eased his hand out of her pants. She was too insensible to speak a word of protest. By the time she came down enough to form a coherent thought, they were both naked and she was wondering how the hell a bookseller had a body like this. Running her hands over the abs she hadn't stopped dreaming about since summer, Cecily decided her comparison to Steve Rogers hadn't been far off the mark. She straddled his body and stretched out, glorying in the feel of all his long, lean muscles as she kissed her way along the tendons of his throat.

"So patient," she murmured, giving a little nip at the shell of his ear, then kissing to soothe the sting.

His hands tightened on her thighs.

"It's one of the things I admire about you. But here's the thing." She wriggled until she could rub the length of him through her slick folds. Definitely not enough. "I'm not."

"Thank Christ." He cupped her nape and pulled her firm against him as he rolled. With one hand, he groped in the nightstand drawer, finally coming up with a condom.

Cecily took it from him, ripping it open and rolling it on. Her eyes met his as she took him in her hand and guided him inside. Reed breathed her name, muscles tensing as he began the slow thrust and retreat, until he filled her completely.

Lowering from his hands to his elbows, he cradled her face. "Okay?"

Pressed skin to skin, body stretched around his, Cecily couldn't contain the radiant smile. "So okay." She laced her hands with his and kissed him.

They began to move, an exquisite torture, riding the edge of pleasure. Skin began to slick and her heart beat hard and fast, in time with the pistoning of his hips. Tension coiled, and she rose higher, her body impossibly light and airy. Joy and love built in equal measure, until full to bursting, she wrapped tight around him and took the leap, carrying him with her.

REED WOKE IN THE CHILL, gray light of dawn and reached for Cecily, thinking they could keep each other warm for another half hour before getting up for work. But his bed was empty. Pushing himself up on one elbow, he frowned. Had it all been a dream? No. He could still smell her on the pillow.

He ran a hand over her side of the bed and found the sheets cold. Had she snuck out in the middle of the night to avoid the walk of shame? Did she have an early meeting she forgot about? They hadn't talked much last night. Was she having regrets? Worse, had she changed her mind about possibly staying?

With a heavy sigh, he flopped back on the bed and scrubbed both hands over his face. This was all too much to contemplate without coffee. As if conjured by the mere thought, the scent of it made his nose twitch. Praying he wasn't hallucinating due to sleep deprivation, Reed rolled out of bed, tugged on some pajama pants and a t-shirt, and shuffled into the living room. He stopped at the edge of the kitchen, momentarily speechless with relief.

She was at the table, feet propped on a chair, with a tiny laptop resting on her bare knees as her fingers flew over the keys. Her hair was a sexy, tumbled mess. He'd done that, and at the sight of it, he wanted to do it all over again. Especially as she wore only his shirt, the sleeves rolled several times to free her hands. He liked seeing her in his space, liked that she'd made herself at home. Seeing her here, like this, it was so easy to imagine her as part of his home.

As if sensing his gaze on her, she looked up. No sexy bedroom eyes here. She looked bright and alert and suspiciously like she may have already downed half a pot of the coffee still on the burner. "Morning."

Reed grunted and shuffled toward the coffee. There would be no coherent speech until the first hit of caffeine. He filled his favorite mug and watched as the heat made the Bat Signal appear on the side. With another jaw-cracking yawn, he joined her at the table, taking in pages of handwritten notes spread over the surface.

"How long have you been up?" he rasped.

"A while," she admitted.

He angled his head, squinting at one of the

sheets, but without his reading glasses, it was hopeless. "What is all this?"

"A business plan."

"You're working on a business plan at the ass crack of dawn? After we were up half the night?" Reed looked at her in suspicion. "You're a *morning* person."

Cecily's lips twitched at the accusation. "My inner body clock does tend to have me up before the sun. But I was too nervous to sleep."

Reed frowned. "Nervous? Are you uncomfortable here?" She didn't look it. But maybe it was the sleepover portion of things that was the problem.

"Not about staying with you. I needed to do some serious thinking, and I couldn't do that all snuggled up with you."

Bracing himself for a serious conversation, Reed drained half his coffee. "Okay."

She set the laptop aside. "When you presented this plan last night, I wanted to jump at it. I don't want to walk away from you, from this."

Her fingers tangled with his on the table, and Reed wished he'd downed all the coffee for fortification. He knew last night had been too fast, too easy. Now that the haze of lust and that initial reaction was past, she was second guessing everything.

"But I can't be reckless about this. I made a very serious mistake once, and it came back to bite both me and my family in the ass. I can't afford to do that again. If I'm going to do this, it has to be a considered decision, one where I've gone through all the details, worked out all the practicalities myself, rather than trusting someone else to do it for me."

Well that stung. Something must've shown on his face because Cecily slipped out of her chair and came around to sit in his lap.

"This has nothing to do with not trusting you. Or Norah, for that matter. It has to do with not trusting myself. I need to be able to justify this to my family, to know that what I'm doing isn't just about what I selfishly want. When they ask me about the logistics, the start up capital, the expected return on investment, I need to have an answer."

Reed softened, sliding his hand around her nape. "They really did a number on you by cutting you out of your non-profit."

"I screwed up."

"You got taken advantage of by someone you cared about," he corrected. "How long are you going to punish yourself for it? How long are they?"

She stiffened. "I'm not—"

"I think you are. I think you've spent the last however many years since the asshole questioning every decision you've made, replaying the whole thing, wondering what signs you missed or how you could've been so blind. And I get that. I get that you got burned and badly. I'm a businessman, so I also understand the need to prove viability of concept, of projecting profits and losses, and crossing all your 't's and dotting all your 'i's. That's just smart. Take what Norah and I put together for you and refine it. Make it fit you and your vision. But do it to make it yours, not because you feel like you have to get permission from someone else."

Cecily sighed and pressed her brow to his. "I have to prove that they can trust me again."

"Why? You're an adult. Out on your own. Earning your own way."

"Because until I do, they'll keep trying to rescue me. Using connections or influence to find me a place that's worthy of a Davenport because they think they know better. I have to prove they can trust me to run my own life so they'll *let me do it*."

Reed wondered what it would take to prove to Cecily that she could trust herself. But that was more than he was capable of thinking about on half a cup of coffee, so he wrapped his arms tighter. "Okay then. So, what's the verdict?"

Her gaze shifted to the papers scattered across the table. "Well, I'm still working on some details, and I need to get some quotes on a few things, but...I think this could really work."

"Good."

He wanted to ask if she was confident enough in that to take the leap, but he wouldn't force this decision. He'd already gotten further in the last twenty-four hours than he'd expected to get in a month. Putting pressure on her for more wouldn't end well. Instead, he changed the subject. "Are you done working on this for a bit?"

"I got most of what was in my head out of it."

"Good. Because we've got an hour before we have to get to work, and I've got a much better idea for how to spend it."

CHAPTER 9

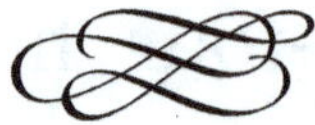

"I HAVE A SURPRISE for you." Cecily could barely contain herself as she cornered Reed in his office.

"Does it involve those two lips meeting these two lips?"

"Totally not the surprise. Though I suspect we'll get there."

"Then lay it on me."

She pulled the copy of the contract out of her purse and laid it on the desk.

He pulled out his horn rims—*swoon*—and proceeded to scan it before his gaze snapped to hers. "This is an offer to purchase real estate. Here."

"It is. Mitch was right. The old train station would make an amazing office. My grandfather has a saying: Start as you mean to continue. If I'm going to make a business here, I might as well start out looking like a real—" But he'd skirted the desk and scooped her up with a whoop before she could finish.

"This is amazing!"

His unfettered enthusiasm curbed the nerves that'd been simmering beneath her excitement. He'd been so reserved the other morning, she hadn't been entirely sure how he'd react.

"The offer hasn't been accepted yet. I lowballed it. The place has been vacant for years, so I figure there's room for negotiation."

"You're so sexy when you talk business. This calls for celebration."

Cecily blocked his mouth with a hand. "Later. I don't have long, I need to get back to the office pretty soon. If you kiss me, you'll just destroy my focus for the rest of the day. I just wanted to drop by and share the news. I need to call Verdant and cancel my interview."

Reed sobered. "Are you *sure* this is what you want?"

She gazed up at him, waiting for the uncertainty, the second guessing. But it never came. Crazy as it was, the decision felt right. "Sometimes you have to take a leap. This is mine."

His eyes warmed. "Okay then. Celebration after work. Whatever you want."

Oh the possibilities. "I'll text you the details."

"Ah. Then I'd best get on over to pick up my replacement phone, post haste." He pulled the cell out of his pocket to show the spiderweb cracks across the screen.

"What happened?"

"Dropped it. Naturally it hit the sidewalk at the *exact* angle needed to totally destroy it. They're holding a replacement for me at the AT&T store in Lawley." He checked his watch. "Which I need to be leaving to go pick up, now that Brenda is back from her lunch break."

"Go ahead. I'll see you tonight. Do you mind if I just use your MacBook to put in some final tweaks to the book signing campaign?"

"Knock yourself out." Reed leaned over and typed in the unlock password. He waited until she took his vacated chair before dropping a quick kiss to her cheek. "Tonight."

As he walked out front to give Brenda instructions, Cecily loosed a dreamy sigh. *Tonight.*

But for a few hours more, she had to bend her brain to work-related tasks. Shoving up her sleeves, she got to work.

Brenda came in as she was loading the remaining newsletter blasts. "I can't believe you're okay with him staying friends with his ex."

Cecily looked up. "Huh?"

"His ex. The one he texts with all the time."

What is she talking about?

"I've met Annelise. He's definitely not talking to her after the way she treated him."

"Not her. That one was a stone-cold bitch. I'm talking about Selina."

Who the hell is Selina?

"He hasn't told you about her, has he?"

Cecily tried to recall if she'd ever heard him mention that name before but drew a blank.

Brenda nodded, as if her silence confirmed it.

Her automatic indictment of Reed annoyed Cecily. "I haven't given him a rundown of all my exes either. It doesn't mean anything."

"Are you all buddy-buddy with any of yours?"

"Well, no, but—"

The older woman rolled right over her protest. "If I were you, I'd want to know what they talk about."

Annoyance and sympathy stirred in equal measure. Cecily wondered if Brenda would ever get to a place where her ugly divorce didn't color everything in her world. She hadn't yet gotten to the point where she realized her over-sharing on the topic made everyone uncom-fortable. "Well, that's understandable given your experience. But Reed's not like that. We're good."

"Suit yourself." Pausing in the doorway, she added, "But I didn't think my ex was like that either."

Cecily stared at the door for several moments after Brenda had gone back down the hall.

I will not *let her make me paranoid. I'm not going to be* that *girl.*

She got back to work. But as she finished with the A-B newsletter groups, what Brenda said continued niggling at her.

Other than Annelise, he'd never mentioned any ex. Certainly he'd have dated people in the intervening years, but no one of any particular significance. He'd have mentioned that. Wouldn't he? As far as she knew, he hadn't been involved with anyone between their almost fling in the summer and now. And even if he had been, they weren't together before, so he had every right to have dated whoever he pleased.

But she couldn't help remembering Jefferson, who'd had a woman on the side. In the grand scheme of things, that'd been the least of his betrayals, so it wasn't something she thought much about. But he'd cheated. People cheated every day. It was a sad fact.

Oh, don't be ridiculous. Reed wouldn't do that.

Even as she thought it, iMessage dinged.

She wasn't going to look, but she saw the name Tony Becker, the author for the big signing. Could be a bump in the road she'd need to smooth out quickly. Just in case, she clicked over.

"Son of a bitch."

Becker was canceling due to a family emergency. *Shit. Shit. Shit. And all the publicity is already out there.*

A part of her brain was already calculating how to deal with that, when she saw the name Selina Kyle in the list of iMessage contacts. The latest message was from earlier that morning. **Wish you'd been able to hear last night's talk from Barry Hanna. He was amazing.**

That was hardly a smoking gun. But she just couldn't stop herself from looking, calling herself an idiot the whole time. She clicked over to the conversation.

Holy shit.

Reed and Selina talked a *lot*. The conversation scrolled back pages and pages. Nothing strange or incriminating, just friendly chat about books and daily life stuff. He'd even talked about her.

Cecily smiled a little. "Master of my craft, huh?"

But as she went back further, she could tell that they were clearly involved at some point. And there was never any change in the tone of their chat to indicate a break up.

Don't be stupid. Reed is absolutely the type who'd break up with someone in person.

But even as the thought occurred to her, she couldn't help but remember all the times she'd seen him texting and smiling. When she'd asked who he was talking to and he'd put her off, saying it was no one important.

The devil on her shoulder whispered in her ear, *There's an easy way to answer this question.*

Her conscience screamed, *Don't do it! This is a violation of his trust and his privacy!*

The devil poked at her conscience with a pitchfork. *And if he's got nothing to hide, then there's nothing to lose. And if he* does *have something to hide...*

"I'm going to hell," Cecily muttered, and clicked in the message box. **You there?** She wished immediately she could take it back.

But the reply was almost instant. **There you are. You've been quiet lately.**

Okay. Okay, you're in it now. Might as well get the answers you're looking for and prepare to grovel and apologize later. **Been busy. Can you do me a favor?**

Selina: **Name it, tiger.**

How to ask this without it coming across as weird? **Define our relationship.**

The laughing emoji came first, followed by Selina's reply. **Got another naysayer because I'm long-distance, huh? Fine. Yes, I exist. Yes,**

I'm your girlfriend. A picture of a cute blonde making a kissy face popped up.

Cecily's head began to roar. **Since when?**

Since beginning of August.

The, **Thanks,** was automatic, though Cecily's hands were trembling.

Selina: **What's this for? Your mom? Tell her she's free to send me a batch of her famous snickerdoodles any time she likes.**

Nausea roiled in her stomach.

August. Selina and Reed had been together since August. Which made *her* the other woman.

Fool me once, shame on you. Fool me twice, shame on me. Clearly her picker was broken, as her cousin Blair would say. And she'd be right.

Oh God. Oh God *how could I have been so stupid? How could I show such horrible judgment again?*

Shoving back from the desk with shaky legs, she gathered her purse and headed for City Hall. *At least I can stop this one in its tracks.*

~

SHIT. Shit. Double shit.

As soon as his new phone was up and running, the first message to pop up was from Tony Becker. Canceling.

Reed had spent the drive back from Lawley getting in touch first with Becker's publicist, then with Tony himself to see if there was any way to talk him out of it. Given the man's mother was going in for double by-pass surgery, that was a great big negative. Reed had offered his prayers without question and told the distraught author he was welcome any time.

Cecily hadn't answered when he'd called to notify her. He figured she'd gone radio silent for a meeting, so he left a voicemail with the news, feeling awful for her. She'd put so much work into this. He hated to see it all go to waste. Not that everything she'd done was a waste. The platform she'd built could be used for future events and promotion for years to come.

He hated to see his own investment go to

waste, too. The outlay on advertising wouldn't hurt him too bad, but he wasn't operating with such a margin of profit that he could afford to have this happen often.

Maybe it's not too late to cancel the ad and get a refund, he mused, stepping back into Inglenook.

"What the holy hell is wrong with you?"

Reed actually stumbled back against the closed door in the face of the fury pumping off Norah as she rose from the couch. Her normally calm and even demeanor had been replaced by a rage so great, he half expected her to bulk up and start screaming "Hulk smash!" And he had no clue what she was so pissed about.

"What?"

"I *trusted* you. I encouraged *her* to trust you. How the hell could you do this to Cecily?"

"Do what? Norah, what the hell are you talking about?"

"You cheated on her, you slimy bastard. I'm ashamed to have to call you family. And you'd better believe that by the time I get through with you, the wrath of God is gonna look like a church picnic."

"I knew it." From the entryway to the next section, Brenda stood, a look of disgust on her face.

Reed shoved away from the door and met Norah toe-to-toe. "What the hell are y'all talking about? I didn't cheat."

"Then who the hell is Selina Kyle and why did she say she's been dating you since August?"

Oh, fuck me. He didn't know how it'd come out. Now was absolutely not the time to ask.

Reed inhaled a long, deep breath and decided he really didn't give a good damn about Brenda's feelings at the moment. "She said it because it's what she was paid to say as part of an invisible girlfriend service I signed up for before Cecily and I got together."

Whatever Norah had been expecting, that wasn't it. Pure bafflement cut through a few levels of her anger. "Invisible girlfriend?"

"Virtual Match is a service that provides an invisible significant other—texts, emails, that kind of thing. People use it to prove they're in a relationship when they're not. It was Zach's idea."

He pulled out his phone and sent Selina a text. **Cat is out of the bag. Please reply back with true details about VM service. It's urgent.**

Her reply came almost at once. **If you're sure...**

Reed: **I'm sure.**

Selina: **I work for Virtual Match as an invisible girlfriend. Reed and I have never met. This is not my real name, not my picture. There was never any real relationship.**

Reed handed the phone to Norah.

"Anybody could say that as a planned cover story," she retorted.

Yanking the phone back, he pulled up his account, handing it over so Norah could see the profile they'd built that night at Los Pantalones.

"How utterly moronic. Why would you need such a thing?"

"It seemed like a way to put a stop to Brenda's inappropriate come-ons without embarrassing us both by actually bringing it up as an issue."

Brenda made a strangled noise and flushed the color of a beet.

"That," Reed said, gesturing toward her. "I was trying to avoid that."

Norah squeezed her temples. "Okay, leaving aside the fact that you're an idiot man, why wouldn't you have canceled the service when you and Cecily got together? Or told her about it and had a good laugh over it?"

"We got to be friends, so I felt bad for firing Selina when she hadn't done anything wrong."

Norah snorted with disgust. "God, that's so you."

"I didn't mention it to Cecily because, frankly, I was a little embarrassed. It was never anything inappropriate and sure as hell never a real relationship. I'd never do that to anyone. How did you even find out about it?"

"Cecily came to me in tears, gave her notice,

and withdrew her offer on the train station property."

Reed felt the blood drain out of his head. "Where is she?"

The last of Norah's anger faded away, leaving sympathy in its wake. "Gone."

"Gone? Gone where?" He'd go after her, explain that he was a dumbass and—

"I don't know. She said she was leaving town."

Reed was already dialing Cecily's cell. Of course she didn't answer. He left another voicemail. "Look, it's me, and nothing is what you think. I didn't cheat on you. Selina's not even a real girl. And okay that sounds ludicrous, but there's an explanation. Please, just...call me back."

The moment he hung up, he looked to Norah. "How long ago was this?"

"A couple of hours."

Maybe she hadn't made it out of town. Reed bolted for the door.

"Reed!"

He turned back at Brenda's shout.

She seemed to deflate, curving in on herself in misery. "I'm sorry."

Reed didn't have time to deal with this. He aimed a finger in her direction. "Stay here and man the store. I'll deal with you later."

Sprinting to his car, he tore through town at speeds that would've gotten him arrested had any of their boys in blue been looking.

Please still be here. Please still be here.

Her car wasn't in the drive when he screeched to a halt. But Christoff's was.

Reed pounded on the door. Christoff opened it, and Reed narrowly avoided the fist the other man led with.

"It's not what you think!"

"What I *think* is that you broke my best friend's heart, you son of a bitch." He landed a firm thump against Reed's shoulder.

"I didn't cheat on her. It's all a misunderstanding." Reed kept his arms up in a defensive position and slowly edged off the porch under Christoff's onslaught.

"I fail to see how that's possible since she heard it from your first girlfriend's mouth."

What? "That can't be possible. Selina is a fake girlfriend. From Virtual Match."

Christoff stopped trying to hit him. "What the hell would you need to use that for?"

"Because Brenda's a cougar and she was after me." And if he'd ever made a more emasculating statement, he couldn't remember it. God.

Christoff cocked a considering head. "Okay, yeah, I can see that. You figured having a fake girlfriend would be less awkward than confronting her about it."

"Yes! Selina isn't real. But Cecily doesn't know that and I have to tell her. Where is she?"

"I wish I knew. She didn't even come home to pack. Just called to tell me she was going."

Panic was starting to claw its way up Reed's throat to strangle him. "When's she coming back?"

Christoff hesitated. "I don't know that she is. She was really upset."

All the starch went out of him, and Reed sank down onto the porch step. Cecily couldn't be gone for good. Surely, she'd come back when he explained.

But how could he explain when there was no way she'd take his calls? She'd probably delete any voicemails or messages or emails from him entirely unread. So unless someone got through to her, explained…she'd go on to… anywhere else that wasn't here.

All because of a woman who wasn't even real.

What have I done?

CHAPTER 10

CECILY CAME TO WAKEFULNESS like a diver rising slowly from the deep. Her body ached and her skull felt stuffed with cotton. But she could hear the rhythmic wash of the sea, and that soothed something soul deep. When she opened her eyes, her face was stiff with salt from dried tears.

The guest room she'd stumbled into near midnight the night before was awash in light that bounced off the white and blue beach cottage decor. Definitely not Dinah's usual style, but Cecily supposed her aunt couldn't be picky when looking for a fully-furnished rental, and beach chic was *de rigueur* in Hilton Head. She slid out of bed and padded over to the window, parting the curtains to look out at the beach.

Pale blue sky bled into silver tipped water far off on the horizon. If a boat had been moored at the little dock, Cecily would've stepped into it, raised the sails, and kept going until she found some solace. She was, after all, a sailor's daughter. But that wasn't practical or feasible. Today was a new day, and she would have to face the thing she'd just run six hundred miles to escape.

Reed Campbell, the man she'd been ready to change her life for, had betrayed her. She'd made yet another crap decision. Picked the wrong man. Again. At least she'd been able to rescind her offer on the train station before the sale went through. This mistake would only affect her. But God, *God* she thought she'd made a better choice this time. She'd learned absolutely nothing. Her judgment, it seemed, was permanently flawed. Cecily knew running wasn't a long-term answer, but she had to get away, had to be able to *think* and decide what was next.

The fist around her heart gave a vicious squeeze.

Okay. Soon. But not yet. She was still in an hour-at-a-time mode. For the next hour, priorities were shower, hydration, and caffeine.

And then she remembered she had nothing but the clothes she'd been wearing and what had been in her car when she bolted.

Great job planning there, Cecily. It occurred to you to stop and get a new cell phone so Reed can't reach you, but not to pick up a toothbrush and clean underwear?

She'd have to go into town later and pick up the basics.

Settling for cleaning her face with a couple of the makeup wipes from her purse, she revised her order of priorities to put caffeine first and headed for the kitchen. As she passed the other spare room, she could hear Dinah's fingers tap tap tapping away on the keys of her laptop. Cecily had been welcomed last night with open arms and no questions, but she knew better than to interrupt now to thank her. The writer at work was an intense creature. Dangerous when provoked.

Dinah kept coffee on until noon, so Cecily found a mug and poured herself a cup before settling into the window seat of the breakfast nook. To keep from falling into a brood, she began mulling over the issue of Tony Becker's canceled book signing. Reed would be out a significant chunk of money. Regardless of their personal issues, she had no desire to see Inglenook fail or the community suffer. Was there some way to turn the marketing at this late date?

"Jesus, honey, you look worse this morning than you did last night."

Startled, Cecily looked up, realizing the half cup of coffee in her hands had gone cold. "Yeah, well, sixteen hours of sobbing will do that to you."

Dinah crossed the room, her bare feet soundless on the tile floor, and grabbed a bottle of water from the fridge. She plucked the mug from Cecily's hands and shoved the bottle into it. "Drink."

"Yes ma'am." Dutifully, Cecily took a slug.

"What's his name?"

"How do you know it's a man?"

"Please. I write romance for a living. I know that look perfectly well. I put it on my heroines' faces on a routine basis—usually with a fair amount of malicious glee. Besides, I just talked to your mother yesterday, so I know everyone in the family is fine. Spill."

"And if I'm not ready to talk about it?"

"Then you crashed at the wrong house. You had last night to keep the trauma to yourself. Now you purge it."

Cecily pouted. "If I'm going to be spilling my heartsblood, can't you at least bribe me with pancakes?"

Dinah's lips twitched. "I suppose I can take that much pity on you." She began moving around the room at lightning speed, and Cecily wondered that the two pencils sticking out of her messy strawberry blonde bun didn't fall.

She took another fortifying glug of water and let the whole story spill out, from their long flirtation, to the weekend at the lake, to how they'd finally gotten together. By the time she got to the damning texts, Dinah slid a plateful of golden, fluffy pancakes in front of her with a bottle of real maple syrup.

"So, let me get this straight. You're head over heels in love with this guy—"

"I never said I was in love with Reed." Her stomach flopped like a beached fish. Just because she hadn't said it, didn't mean it wasn't true.

Dinah rolled her eyes. "Yes, you did. You just didn't use those exact words. Anyway, you're in love with him, and at the first real test of your relationship, you cut and run?"

"Excuse me? He *cheated* on me. Or, no," Cecily corrected, "apparently he cheated *with* me since it seems she was with him first."

"Says a girl you don't know in a series of

text messages that you didn't even stick around to talk to him about. Come on, Cecily, this is not the kind of shero you are. At the very least you should've had the moxie to confront him."

"Well, I'm sorry to disappoint you by not being as brave as the women in your books."

"Oh, don't be ridiculous. You're every bit as brave as they are. But that's not the point. You don't come to me to sugar coat things. You come because I'll tell you the hard truths. And the truth I'm hearing is that cheating doesn't fit at all with the actions of the man you've described to me. In my experience, when things seem out of character, it's because I don't know the character as well as I thought I did or there are circumstances I wasn't aware of. In your case, I'd say because of that fiasco in college and the fact that you hide who you are and don't let yourself get close, you don't know everything there is to know about Reed."

"You've just made my point. I didn't think he was the kind of guy who'd cheat."

"You're misunderstanding me entirely. I'm

saying there's more to the story."

"I don't know how else it can be interpreted, Aunt D."

"You need to talk to him, if for no other reason than to call him out. You're not going to find out any other way."

Cecily shook her head. "I don't want to talk to him. Not yet, anyway."

"Don't you want to find out that you're wrong?"

"I'd be ecstatic to find out I'm wrong. But I thought I was wrong about Jefferson, too, and we see how that turned out."

"Jefferson was a complete ass, and you're well rid of him."

Cecily could hardly argue differently. "At this point, I just want to go to my interview in San Francisco at the end of the week with as clear a head as possible. I don't want things with Reed cluttering up my mind."

"And you really think not dealing with this is the way to a clear head?"

"It's the only way, right now."

Dinah narrowed her blue eyes and pursed her lips in disgust.

Cecily laid down her fork. "Okay, you know what? Fine. I'll make you a deal. The author we set up the signing for canceled at the last minute—it's too late to pull most of the publicity, but it's not too late for me to change the who. I've got remote access to everything. You go to Wishful in Tony Becker's place. You meet Reed and get your own feel for him. You've got good instincts, and I know you'll pull no punches. If you still think he deserves a chance to explain, then I'll talk to him after my interview." Her notoriously reclusive aunt would never agree to that.

Now those narrowed eyes took on an intrigued gleam. "You want me to go do a last-minute signing at your boyfriend's bookstore?"

Cecily huffed. "He's not—"

"Fine." Dinah held up her hand like a traffic cop. "When is the signing scheduled?"

She gaped. Dinah was going to *go?* "Day after tomorrow. Seven P.M. at Inglenook."

"Okay. Get me the address."

As she picked up her fork again, Cecily reflected that absolutely nothing was going as she'd planned.

CHRISTOFF HAD TAKEN pity on Reed.

"It's a last-ditch effort, but I'd say you're desperate enough to try it."

It was true, so Reed hadn't argued the point. Instead, he'd taken the first flight he could find to get him to Greenwich.

Now he looked up at the house sitting at the address Christoff had given him. House was really a misnomer. Mansion was probably putting it mildly. He was looking at a full-on estate. And judging by the number of vehicles parked out front, he'd arrived in the middle of something.

His phone buzzed with an incoming text.

Selina: **Make it yet?**

Through the long hours of waiting in assorted airports, he'd texted her the whole story. She'd kept him focused instead of completely freaking out.

Reed: **Yeah. This may have been a mistake.**

Selina: **You've come this far. The worst they can do is throw you out.**

Reed: **That isn't a comfort.**

But he put his rental into gear and drove up the long drive to the house.

A big van with *Simply Elegant* written out in script along the side was surrounded by people unloading in a steady stream. He parked where he hoped he'd be out of the way and tried to figure out who he should ask. Scratch that. He didn't even know exactly *what* he should ask. A smart man would've planned that out somewhere in all the hours he'd spent sitting in airports for his three connecting flights. Reed had spent that time continually trying Cecily's cell and trying to craft an appropriate apology and explanation. At least until her voicemail was full. Probably evidence she'd turned off her phone.

Reed poked his head around the open back of the van, looking for somebody to ask who was in charge, and found a large box thrust into his hands.

"Take those to the kitchen," the man inside ordered, already turning to grab the next box.

Reed started to say something about not being part of the crew, but he seemed to be gumming up the steady rhythm the group had established, so he turned to follow the other workers through the front door. Despite the soaring entryway, he was struck by how much the house felt like a home the moment he walked inside. The banister of the long staircase looked like the kind kids had slid down. The wide expanses of glossy wood floors were covered in faded rugs—no doubt expensive and high quality, but used. Nothing about the place had the brittle, don't-touch air he'd expect of a place like this.

He trailed the person in front of him down a hall, through a wide living room done up in leather and comfortable fabrics and more of those antiques that actually got used, and finally into an enormous kitchen. A woman in a slim black skirt and white shirt was barking out orders. At her direction, Reed added his box of dishes to a growing pile in one corner of the room.

"Excuse me," he said.

At his accent, she stopped speaking, perfectly manicured brows going up. "You are not from around here."

"No, ma'am. I'm not on the crew. I'm actually looking for someone. Cecily Dixon?"

"Who wants to know?"

Reed turned and immediately knew where Cecily had learned that regal air. "Mrs. Dixon?"

She tipped her head slightly in acknowledgment, her eyes—the same as Cecily's—not welcoming but not cold either.

Reed wished he'd taken the time to get a hotel so he could've showered and changed out of his rumpled clothes. But as he'd been taught, impeccable manners made up for a lot. He crossed over to her. "Ma'am. My name is Reed Campbell. I'm

—" After what had happened, he could hardly call himself Cecily's boyfriend. "—looking for Cecily."

His name didn't seem to ring any bells, which made him wonder whether she'd ever even mentioned him.

"You're from Mississippi." It wasn't a question.

"Yes, ma'am."

"Then you should know she's in Wishful."

Damn it. She wasn't here. Reed took a breath. "No ma'am, she's not at the moment. I was hoping you'd know where she is. It's rather urgent that I locate her."

"Urgent enough that you'd take a chance that she'd be here?" That seemed to intrigue her.

"Christoff and Norah suggested I try it. She's not taking my calls at the moment. Or, apparently, anybody else's. We're getting worried."

"Norah Burke?"

"Yes, ma'am. She's about to be my cousin by

marriage." Why he said that, he had no idea, except that it was instinctive to talk connections and who his people were.

"Why don't you come with me?" she suggested. "Hilary, I believe you have things well in hand here?"

"Yes, Mrs. Dixon," said the woman in the black skirt.

"Have some coffee sent to the sunroom, please. And find Frank."

Hilary nodded.

Reed followed Cecily's mother to another room facing the expansive view of gardens behind the house. Out the wide windows across the back, he could see a massive tent set up on the lawn. Tables were being set up beneath it by more of the bustling staff.

"I'm interrupting something. I apologize for the intrusion and for stopping by unannounced."

Mrs. Dixon waved that off and took a seat in one of the padded wicker chairs. "Please, sit.

Have you been traveling all night, Mr. Campbell?"

"Yes, ma'am." He sat and gestured outside, trying to buy himself a little time to think. "What is all this?"

"A fundraising gala for the Hero's Help Alliance. We were hoping Cecily would come home for it, as the organization was her brainchild."

"A bit late for that, isn't it?" Reed asked, then wanted to bite his tongue as her brows rose.

"I beg your pardon?"

Well, he was in it now. "Y'all pretty neatly cut her out, so why would she want to come back and have her biggest failure thrown in her face?"

Mrs. Dixon looked truly shocked. "Failure? The Alliance wasn't a failure."

"She thinks it was. She thinks she let the whole family down because of what that—" Reed managed to cut the profanity short. "Of what her ex did."

"We don't blame her for the actions of that

asshole." This came from the doorway.

The speaker was a tall man with silver shot hair the same dark shade as Cecily's. Her father, Reed figured. Beside him, a tall, willowy girl looked Reed up and down in blatant curiosity.

"She thinks you do," Reed said quietly. "She's spent the last few years working her tail off to become the best in her field because she wants to feel worthy of the family name again."

Mr. Dixon stepped into the room. "I'm sorry, who are you?"

Reed rose and offered his hand to the other man, but before he could speak, the girl interrupted, "You're him."

"Sorry?"

"Bookstore guy. The reason she doesn't want to leave Mississippi."

"Blair?" he guessed.

She nodded.

"I'm Reed. And at the moment I'm the reason she *did* leave Mississippi. But she's got bad information, and I have to talk to her. Do you know where she is?"

Blair shook her head. "I haven't talked to her in several days. But when I did she was happy. What did you do?"

He absorbed the accusation as another woman came in with a coffee service. "Not what she thinks I did." In his pocket, his phone began to ring. He pulled it out to check the read out and saw it was the bookstore. "I'm sorry, I need to take this." Reed hit answer. "Is she back?"

There was a hesitation on the other end before Brenda said, "No, she's not back. That's not why I'm calling."

"Then whatever it is can wait."

"No, it can't. Did you get Dinah McClure to agree to a signing here?"

Reed blinked. "No. Why would you think that?"

"Because all our social media accounts say that she is. The streams are blowing up. Everybody's telling everybody. There are people coming all the way from Jackson to attend the alleged signing. *Tonight.* The only person in the romance community who might stir up an even bigger fuss would be Nora Roberts."

"This doesn't make any sense. Have you checked Dinah McClure's social media to see if there's any corroboration?" Reed was aware of something shifting in the room behind him, but couldn't stop to analyze it.

"She's a well-known recluse. She doesn't *do* social media."

"Well, she's not coming, so we need to take it down. It's bad enough Becker had to cancel. If people think somebody as prestigious as Dinah McClure is taking his place and show up to nothing, they're gonna be furious."

"I can't take it down," Brenda said.

"Why not?"

"All the passwords have been changed. I'm locked out of the accounts entirely."

He frowned. "Are you sure the caps lock key wasn't on? Maybe you exceeded the number of incorrect logins."

"I know the passwords, Reed. The only way we could be locked out is if Cecily locked us out on purpose. I think you need to face the fact that she's done this in retaliation."

"No. No way would Cecily endanger my business because she's angry at me. She's not a vengeful woman."

Except he knew she could be when properly provoked. She'd gone after Norah's asshole ex to garner a confession and taken on Annelise purely to put her in her place. She'd said herself she had an overdeveloped sense of justice. He'd just only been aware of it in conjunction with protecting the people she cared about. Still, he couldn't imagine her trying to tank his business.

But what other explanation could there be? The passwords didn't change themselves. The social media content didn't spontaneously morph from a midlist author to one of the biggest names in publishing. In ten hours, they were going to be besieged by customers who would think they'd pulled some kind of bait-and-switch.

Reed felt a little sick.

Brenda's voice was small. "I'm sorry things turned out like this. I'm sorry I pushed you into doing something that led to her walking away."

He sighed, shoving a hand through his hair. There was no sense in staying pissed at Brenda when the blame lay squarely on his own shoulders. "It's not your fault. There were a dozen points I could have done things differently and didn't. That's not on you. Let's just deal with this however we can."

"What are you going to do?" In the background, he could hear the shop bell jingle as someone opened the door.

He shook his head, not that she could see. "Hell if I know. Make signs? Put up fliers? Norah might be able to put something out on the city's social media. But it won't get everybody." Cecily was too damned good at her job for them to undo this. And maybe that had been the point. To give him some kind of crisis to deal with so he couldn't possibly come after her right now. Except here he was, over a thousand miles from home.

"Excuse me, I'm looking for Reed Campbell," a muffled voice said.

Brenda made some kind of *eep* and began to stammer. "I…um…he's…here."

There was a rustle and then the new voice came on the line. "Mr. Campbell?"

"Yes? How can I help you?"

A rich chuckle rolled. "Oh, Mr. Campbell, the correct question is how I can help you."

"Who is this?"

"Dinah McClure."

Reed actually pulled the phone away from his ear to stare at it, as if that would allow him to see into his bookstore. "Am I being punked?"

"Far from it. I am here for both rescue and reconnaissance."

Did anything this woman said make actual sense?

Evidently copping to his cluelessness, she spelled it out for him. "Cecily sent me to rescue your signing."

"Is she all right? Where is she? I need to talk to her."

"Calm down. She's safe. As to all right, that's a far more subjective question."

He sank back into a chair and scrubbed a hand over his face. Okay. Okay, that was a start. And the fact that Cecily had—even when furious with him and hurt beyond belief—sought to help him with his business, had to mean something. Didn't it?

"Now if you'll come on in to the store, I'll be happy to talk more with you about all this while I sign stock for tonight's reading."

Aware of everyone's gaze on him, he struggled to pull himself together. "I'm afraid that's not possible. I'm in Greenwich."

"Are you now?" Dinah purred. "Are you still at the estate?"

"I—yes."

"Put me on speaker," she ordered. "I want to say hi to Genevieve."

"Who?"

"Cecily's mother, darling."

The world had gone absolutely mad. But Reed did as she ordered.

"Jen?"

"Hello, Dinah," said Mrs. Dixon.

"Hey Aunt D!" Blair called.

Aunt? This woman was related to Cecily?

"Dinah," Mr. Dixon said.

"Oh wonderful, the gang's all here," Dinah said. "I assume Cecily hasn't called."

"She hasn't," Mrs. Dixon said.

"Never does when she's licking her wounds. She's fine. Well, not fine, but safe."

Everybody looked at Reed. He felt like an idiot sitting here with his phone on speaker and most of Cecily's family staring him down. "Look, Ms. McClure—"

"Dinah."

"Dinah, I don't know what Cecily told you—"

"Plenty." There was a wealth of things unsaid in her tone.

No doubt. "She has everything wrong. I'd never, ever hurt her deliberately, and if she'd just *talk* to me, give me a chance to explain, I can clear all of this up."

"I suspected there was more to the story than she knew. She was far less inclined to hear it than I. Hence the reconnaissance portion of my mission. So, while your lovely shop keeper here is handing me those books—my publisher has overnighted more, by the way—you tell us your side of things. If, by the end, I'm satisfied that you deserve her instead of to be castrated without anesthesia, we'll talk about what I can do to help you fix this." Her pleasant tone held an underlying message that said *I take no shit so don't lie to me.*

He'd come prepared to tell Cecily everything. To grovel, as necessary. Looking around at all the expectant faces, Reed realized these were the gatekeepers, and if he stood a chance in hell of getting to talk to her again, he'd have to start with all of them.

He took a breath. "It all started because I hate confrontation…"

CHAPTER 11

WHY HASN'T DINAH CONTACTED *me?*

The same question had been circling through Cecily's mind for hours. The sleepless night she'd had in the wake of the book signing was written beneath her eyes. It'd taken all of her considerable skill with cosmetics to mask the exhaustion and mime bright-eyed enthusiasm for her interview at Verdant.

Unfortunately, her distractability wasn't as easy a thing to cover up. She'd gone through the entire tour in a daze. The only thing she'd successfully absorbed was that Verdant was a competitive workplace that rewarded innovation. That and they had nap rooms. Like Google. It'd taken every shred of self-control she possessed not to beg for the opportunity to crawl into one before facing the panel interview with all five partners. Instead, she'd ducked into the restroom to check her phone one last time.

Still nothing.

What did Dinah's silence *mean?* That there was more to the story? That Dinah was on the fence? Or that the news was bad and she didn't want to deliver it before Cecily's interview?

Put me out of my misery already!

But Dinah's telepathy was clearly on the fritz because no answer was forthcoming by the time Cecily had to join the partners in the conference room. She bought herself a little more time to pull herself together by accepting the offer of coffee. But all too soon, she took her seat at the head of a conference table overlooking the vast, glassed-in atrium at Verdant, surrounded by all five partners of the firm.

"Tell us about your time at Helios," Nina Winslow invited.

Easy peasy.

"It's one of the most coveted internships in Chicago. The one all the first year grad students hear about almost from day one. Once I got there and began working under Norah Burke, I understood why." Cecily told them about the various accounts she'd worked on, the contributions she'd made to the team. She waited for the fizz of accomplishment, the rush she'd felt working on those projects, but the whole thing felt like a recitation of someone else's life. Coming back to corporate marketing was going to be pretty jarring after what she'd been doing in Wishful.

Gavin Sheppard consulted his notes. "I understand you left Helios before your internship was complete. Can you tell us why?"

Because I blackmailed Norah's ex into retracting the smear campaign his father started against her. Yeah, no, she couldn't mention that.

"Norah left Helios in January and relocated

to Wishful, Mississippi. We have an exceptional working relationship, so I felt that my apprenticeship would be better served by continuing to work with her, rather than switching horses midstream, as it were."

"And what exactly have you been doing in Mississippi?" asked Derek—something. Cecily couldn't remember his last name. She could tell he couldn't fathom that she'd done anything of import in a place so small.

Feeling defensive on Norah's behalf and protective of Wishful, Cecily squared her shoulders. "We waged a war and turned the tide of a town that's been economically disadvantaged for several decades—without resorting to accepting the less than beneficial offer of GrandGoods, which would've irrevocably damaged the character of Wishful." Warming to her topic, Cecily continued, "And since they got sent packing, we've firmly established the first phase of a long-term rural tourism campaign, while assisting individual local businesses in maximizing their potential."

As she began to outline the specifics of the rural tourism campaign, Cecily's new phone beeped with an incoming text. Mortification at her unprofessionalism was quickly chased away by the twin demons of hope and dread. They seemed to circle her as she muttered an apology and reached for the phone to switch it over to vibrate—and saw the text from Dinah.

Plot twist! Talk to him.

Cecily blinked at the message, her train of thought entirely derailed. What had Dinah found out? *Plot twist?* In Dinah's world, that meant something wasn't as it seemed—exactly as she'd predicted. Her aunt was no bullshitter when it came to matters of the heart. That meant that somehow, some way, there was *some* kind of explanation for what Cecily had seen. She couldn't fathom what that was, but hope flared in her chest nonetheless. That meant everything could be all right. Didn't it?

"Is everything okay?" Nina asked.

"Yes." Cecily thumbed the phone to silent

and mentally shook herself. "I'm terribly sorry. Where was I?"

"The planned roll out of Phase Two."

"Ah, yes. Phase Two deals with the revitalization of other downtown retail space in preparation for luring small business entrepreneurs. Part of that is individual marketing plans for the existing businesses, maximizing their client base and revenues. That's predominantly what I've been doing the last several months." She began to describe some of the specific projects she'd spearheaded. As she got into the meat of those campaigns, citing befores and afters, Cecily realized that nothing she'd ever done at Helios—even while under Norah's tutelage—had ever made her this happy.

On the heels of that epiphany, Gavin asked, "Why don't you tell us about your vision about marketing in general."

"I come from a family that believes in utilizing skills in the service of others. In light of that, I love connecting on an individual level—with both clients and their customer base. That personal service is so rewarding. And I suppose my vision is of doing that in a way that's afford-able for small businesses." Which was exactly the business plan she'd outlined for her own firm.

As she looked around the table at the faces of these movers and shakers, Cecily tried to imagine herself as one of them. She tried to see the life she'd envisioned for so long. And she simply couldn't. The truth was, no matter how things turned out with Reed, she didn't want to work in corporate marketing. No matter how prestigious.

"This firm is one of the best in the country. But Verdant doesn't do small. You have a dif-ferent vision, a different function, and I'm not sure I'm the best fit for that. I appreciate the honor of interviewing with you more than you can know, but I've got another path to follow."

The various stunned faces around the table made it quite clear that no one had ever walked away from the opportunity of a job with their firm.

"Well, we appreciate your candor, Miss Dixon." Nina offered her hand.

Cecily took it. "I apologize for taking up your time."

"Not at all. Your unique viewpoint is…refreshing. And should you change your mind, give me a call."

She knew she wouldn't be changing her mind. Not on this. "Thank you for the opportunity."

"I'll walk you out."

As they descended the spiral staircase down to the first floor, Nina asked, "Where will you be headed?"

Cecily thought of Wishful and of the confrontation waiting there. "Home."

"Best of luck. I suspect you'll be successful at whatever you put your mind to."

She certainly hoped so.

The moment Nina Winslow left her side, Cecily pulled her phone back out and dialed Reed's number from memory. It began to ring as she stepped outside. It rolled to voicemail.

Damn it. She'd expected him to pick up. What the hell should she say?

"I—Reed, it's Cecily. I have a new number. I'd like to talk to you. Call me back." She unzipped her purse, feeling deflated and losing some of her nerve.

A figure straightened from the wall lining the courtyard. "Hey, Peanut."

She stumbled to a halt. "Dad? What are you *doing* here?"

"Since you've gone incommunicado, I thought it best if I caught you out here." He pulled her into a tight hug, and Cecily burrowed in, needing the comfort of family.

"Sorry about that. Life got…"

"Complicated?" he suggested.

Understatement of the year. She pulled back. "Is everything okay at home?"

"Oh sure. The gala was a big success."

She'd forgotten that was last night. Even though she hadn't actually wanted to go, hadn't wanted to face any of the people she'd disappointed, she still felt a pang. At least the people who'd taken over in her stead had made a success of her vision. "Glad to hear it."

"Why don't we go get some coffee and have a chat," her father suggested.

He obviously had something on his mind or he wouldn't have flown across the country to see her. But Cecily knew him. Frank Dixon wouldn't get to whatever it was until he was good and ready, so she fell into step beside him, hunching her shoulders against the chill, gray day. They strolled in companionable silence to a nearby coffee shop, saying nothing until they'd placed their orders and claimed a booth by the window.

"So how did your interview go?"

How to answer that question? "The interview itself went fine. I just don't think the position is a good fit."

Her dad nodded. "Seems like that's been happening with a lot of the possible options for jobs since you finished grad school."

"I'm not dragging my feet, Dad, I swear. I just—"

He laid a hand over hers. "I never said you were. Stop putting words in my mouth. I'm not pushing you into anything, just making an observation."

They each settled back in their seats. Cecily wracked her brain, trying to think of some way to explain what she wanted to do that the family would accept.

"You know, there's nothing wrong with not being sure of exactly what you want to do right now. Few people land in exactly the perfect career straight out of the gate."

"That's not the problem. I do know what I want to do."

"Then what *is* the problem?"

Cecily bit her lip. "I don't think the family is going to like it."

"So what?"

She couldn't have heard him right. "What?"

"So what? I mean, provided you aren't planning on becoming an exotic dancer or something, why does it matter what the family thinks? It's your life, Peanut."

"Because I'm a Davenport."

"You're as much a Dixon as a Davenport. And Dixons have no problem making their own way." He leaned forward, eyes intent on hers. "Don't live your life based on what you think the family expects. The *only* thing any of us expects—and I include Cecil in this—is for you to do work you love, that you value. Just because most of us happen to do that within one of the arms of the Davenport holdings doesn't mean you have to. You have nothing to prove. To us or anyone else. You have *nothing* to make up for."

Cecily's throat went thick with unshed tears. If she could've scripted what she wanted to hear from her family, this wouldn't have been too far off. She swallowed past the lump. "How…How did you even know I was worried about all of this?"

"First, tell me what it is you really want to do. Even if that's coming back to head the Alliance. Because that's on the table if you want it."

She stared at him for a long moment. She'd already said no in the interview at Verdant. She'd already decided on this path. There was no reason not to tell him.

"I want to open my own marketing firm. In Wishful."

"Tell me about it."

So she did. For near half an hour, she told him her vision, outlining her business plan in detail. He was smiling by the end.

"It's a solid plan. And it suits you down to the ground."

"You really think so?"

"I do. Why Wishful? Because Norah's there?"

"That's part of it. And I'm already hooked into the community. I've already been a part of the changes, and it just makes sense to stay and see the rest of it through."

"Sensible," he conceded. "I kinda wondered if Reed Campbell might have something to do with it."

Cecily almost bobbled her coffee mug. "How do you know anything about Reed?"

"He came to see us yesterday."

"He did *what?*"

"Well, more properly, he came to see you, but you weren't there."

"Reed came to Greenwich?"

"He did. Seems you blew town pretty upset the other day and he was pretty damned worried about you. Enough to take three different flights to get up to us on the off chance you'd run home."

"How did he even know where to go?"

"Christoff."

If Christoff had given him the address, that was an even bigger sign that there was some kind of explanation for Selina Kyle. When was he going to call her back?

"Things are up in the air with Reed at the moment," she hedged.

"That's all obviously between the two of you, but for what it's worth, we all liked him."

"All?"

"Me, your mother, and Blair. He held up really well to the full court press. Including Dinah via speakerphone."

Cecily didn't even want to imagine how that had gone.

"We found him polite, well-spoken and entirely willing to own up to his mistakes and grovel."

"Did he tell you what those mistakes were?"

"Yes, but that's something you need to hear from him."

Cecily studied her dad. "You're not warning me off."

"He seems like an honorable guy. And he's in love with you. You specifically. He doesn't give a damn about the Davenport legacy, the connections, or the money. Though he wasn't intimidated by them either. As far as I'm concerned, that places him miles ahead of everybody you've ever dated."

"I think," she said slowly, "that I've misjudged him." Again.

Her father tipped back the last of his coffee. "Then it looks like you've got a plane to catch."

"I'm going to miss Dinah," Brenda sighed.

"She was only here for two days," Reed pointed out. And in the thirty-six hours he'd been around her, she'd exhausted him with questions about Virtual Match for a prospective new book. He figured he owed her, both for lobbying on his behalf with Cecily and for the incredibly successful signing. But after the last few days, he was ready for life to go back to normal.

"I know, but she's so amazing. We stayed up half the night after the signing drinking and talking."

Reed didn't know what Dinah had said to Brenda, but she seemed calmer, less hostile than he'd seen her in all the time she'd worked for him, and just generally in a better place.

He wished he were in a better place.

He'd gotten Cecily's message that she wanted to talk, but when he'd returned her call at the new number, she hadn't answered or called him back. What the hell did that mean? Was she traveling? Had she changed her mind?

A part of him wanted to text Selina to ask her opinion, but he'd finally canceled Virtual Match yesterday

"We should start sorting out who our next author will be," Brenda continued. "Dinah will be a tough act to follow, of course, but the newsletter sign ups have gone through the roof. People are going to start looking to Inglenook as a hub for—"

She broke off as the shop bell jangled.

Reed looked toward the door and went still as Cecily strode in, shoulders hunched against the cold. His heart leapt into a frantic tattoo, and it was all he could do not to bolt to take her in his arms. She looked road weary, faint lines of strain bracketing her mouth. Her long, dark hair was plaited in a loose braid over one shoulder. She paused in the entryway, eyes meeting his. He couldn't read her expression and that terrified him about what she'd come to say.

With a visible breath, she squared her shoulders and made for the counter.

"Cecily, I'm so sor—" Brenda began, but Cecily cut her off with a hand.

"This is between me and Reed. If you could excuse us."

Brenda looked between the two of them.

"We'll be in the kitchen," Reed said, making an after you gesture toward the back.

Cecily swept by him, saying nothing even when he shut the door behind them.

"You want coffee?" he asked.

"I'm pretty sure my blood coffee level is outside the legal limit already. I've been traveling since yesterday afternoon. Took longer to get back from San Francisco than I'd hoped."

Then she'd kept the interview with Verdant. The hope that had ignited at the sight of her began to fizzle. But she'd sent him Dinah. She'd called and said they needed to talk. She'd come back, so obviously she was willing to hear him out. If there was a chance in hell that she'd forgive him, he'd do anything he had to in order to make this work.

Cecily leaned back against the counter, arms crossed. "Okay. I'm ready to listen."

Not knowing how else to start, he pulled two sheets of folded paper out of his pocket and handed them over. "Go ahead. Read it."

She read the first page, frowning. "I don't understand. What am I looking at?"

"That is my account record for Virtual Match and the profile of my virtual girlfriend, Selina Kyle, whom I named after the alter ego of Catwoman."

Her perfectly manicured brows shot up. "*Virtual* girlfriend?"

From the look on her face, Reed could tell she was wondering what kind of freaktastic geek thing that was.

"It's a service for people who need fake significant others for whatever reason. To keep their nosy grandma from setting them up with somebody. To stop the unceasing questions about who they're dating. To keep well-intentioned folks from trying to convince you that you need to get back out there after a breakup when you're just not ready. Whatever. In my case, Selina was a shield against Brenda. As you know, Brenda had a hideous divorce, and shortly after I hired her, she came onto me. I didn't want to hurt her feelings or give her more rejection, so I concocted a fake girlfriend using this service, in order to get her to back off. And it worked."

"You're telling me that I successfully had a conversation with a *computer?*"

"No, it's a real person on the other end. That's the genius of the service. I didn't tell you about it because I felt kind of embarrassed about the whole thing. It happens that whoever is playing Selina became a friend. And I know it's stupid, but I didn't feel right about firing my friend when you and I got together, so I didn't." He took a step toward her. "I'm sorry, Cecily. I can't tell you how sorry I am that I hurt you, even unintentionally. Norah, Christoff, and Dinah have already informed me of all the ways in which I am a complete dumbass. Between the three of them, they've probably covered them all, but you're welcome to take all your best shots. I owe that to you at least."

Her throat worked and she shook her head, eyes going suspiciously shiny. "I don't want to take a shot."

Reed's stomach sank. He was too late.

But then she shoved away from the counter and launched herself into his arms, and he thought nothing had ever felt so wonderful as the staggering impact of her slamming into him. Her voice was muffled against his chest. "I'm so sorry I doubted you. Again."

She forgave him. She understood. Relief almost took him out at the knees as all the stress and strain and worry of the past week drained away. He held on tight and rocked her, beyond grateful that this main hurdle was past them. But it wasn't the only one. "Yeah, well, even I admit the evidence looked pretty damning. I don't blame you for doubting. In your shoes, I'd have kept the interview, too."

At the reminder, she stiffened.

Reed rushed on before she could say anything. "Listen. It's fine. I get it. You need to take the job. It's the best thing for your career. So I'll come with you to San Francisco."

Cecily pulled back to look up at him in shock. "You'd give up Inglenook?"

Reed didn't hesitate. "Brenda's trained well enough to run things, and I can always hire more staff to help in my absence. I can find a bookstore to manage anywhere. I can't find another you, and if I let you go, I'll regret it for the rest of my life. I love you."

Her lips quirked, "I kinda thought you might since you tried to chase me down like one of the heroes in Dinah's books. You went to Greenwich."

They'd told her then.

"I did. I was desperate to find you and explain."

"You faced the third degree from almost my entire family."

"It wasn't that bad." At her *Really?* look he

said, "Well okay, I had a moment or two with your dad while I was explaining everything, and the fact that Dinah was on speakerphone the whole time was kind of terrifying, but I made it out with all my limbs intact."

"You told Dinah about all this?"

"Yeah. She asked about a million questions about how the service works. I'm pretty sure she got a plot bunny out of the whole thing."

Cecily's lips twitched. "That would be just like her."

"She's a force of nature, your aunt. Or ex-aunt? I wasn't entirely clear on how y'all are related."

"She used to be married to my uncle. We stayed close. She likes you. They all like you. In fact, Dad came out to San Francisco to talk to me after he saw you."

Had Reed really found an ally in Frank Dixon? "What did he say?"

"He reminded me of something yesterday that I've spent way too much time forgetting. I'm every bit as much a Dixon as a Davenport.

And the thing is? Dixons are decisive. We know what we want and we go after it."

Reed's heart kicked up. "Yeah? What do you want?"

"You." Cecily stepped back into him, framing his face between her palms. "I turned Verdant down."

"You did?" Relief slid through him, followed by complete, dumbfounded shock. "You turned them down even without knowing the truth about Selina?"

"Yeah," she admitted. "I mean, maybe they wouldn't have offered me a job anyway, but I realized corporate marketing isn't going to make me happy. I didn't come alive in that interview until I started talking about the small business campaigns I've worked on in Wishful. *That* makes me happy. And I would never have realized that without you. I'd never have been willing to go after that without you."

"I just gave you an option." An option he'd hoped would work for her, but one he'd given up hope she'd take when things blew up between them.

"You helped me to see past the duty I felt I owed my family. So I'm coming home and opening my own firm, exactly like we talked about. I want small business marketing, and I want Wishful."

Home. She'd called Wishful home. She'd chosen this life, this town, even without knowing where they stood. This was what she truly wanted. The vise that'd been cranked tight around his chest for days finally loosened, and he could breathe again. No more ticking time clock. No more artificial end to what was between them. They could slow down and enjoy the ride.

"Thank God."

And as he lowered his lips to hers, drowning in the sweetness of having things finally set to rights between them, Reed found that slow was the last thing he wanted.

"MR. MCGEE WILL SEE you now."

Cecily rose from her chair in the waiting room of McGee, Buckley, and Connelly and followed the receptionist down the hall. Tucker McGee, the original Phil Davis in Wishful Community Theater's production of *White Christmas,* walked around his desk to greet her, no limp in evidence.

"All the paperwork is drawn up. We just need to get your signature."

Cecily peered down at his dress shoes as she followed him over to the conference table.

Tucker went over the contracts, and she signed her name approximately a million times.

"That's the last one. I'll have Margaret make a copy for you. We'll be taking it down to the courthouse for filing later this afternoon." He rose and called to the receptionist, hanging over the freshly signed contracts.

"Okay, I have to ask. Where's your cast?"

"I was misdiagnosed," he said easily.

She arched a brow. "How do you get misdiagnosed with a broken leg?"

His expression settled somewhere between smug and sheepish as he returned to his seat. "I decided my understudy needed the part more."

Cecily thought back to the gossip she'd heard surrounding the play, about how Tucker had broken his leg, shoving Brody into his role as leading man. What a delightful twist. "Needed the opportunity to get the girl, you mean." She laughed. "And people talk about how Norah arranges things to suit her."

"They say the same thing about you, and now they'll say it more often." Tucker handed over the keys. "Congratulations, Cecily, you are, officially, the new owner of the Wishful train depot."

She clutched them in her fist and resisted the urge to do a little jig. That could wait until she was in the privacy of her new office building. "Thanks, Tucker."

Gathering up her copy of the paperwork, Cecily said goodbye and stepped out into the frigid December day. Before sliding on her gloves, she sent a quick text to Reed. **Finally done.**

His response was immediate. **Meet you there.**

She could've taken her car, but the building was only a few blocks from Tucker's office, and she wanted to walk through the town she'd adopted as her own. Wreaths and holiday banners adorned all the streetlights downtown. A massive Christmas tree reached toward the sky on the green just in front of City Hall. Shop windows all along the way held cheerful displays inviting shoppers to come inside. Cecily knew most of them would be offering hot chocolate or mulled cider to entice shoppers into lingering. It pleased her that most of the parking spaces were filled and people strolled along the streets, hands full of shopping bags. Two weeks to Christmas and downtown Wishful was doing a brisk business. The knowledge that she'd helped make that a reality warmed her against the chill.

By January, she'd be doing the same from her new firm instead of under the loose auspices of the city planner. Maybe February. It depended on how long it took her to get the building cleaned up and turned into something resembling an actual office. The city had cleaned out all the junk they'd been storing there for the past twenty-odd years, but it was a long way from ready for clients. She'd considered renovating to the specs Mitch Campbell had drawn up for Norah, but much as she loved the design, she didn't want to dip any further into her trust fund than she had to purchase the building. She preferred to let things grow organically, see what she could make of it on her own. And that meant she needed to get creative. Still, Whistle Stop Marketing was close to becoming a real thing.

She couldn't wait.

The bright flash of yellow at the front door had Cecily slowing.

What on earth?

Pansies. Two enormous blue-glazed pots of bright faced pansies and some kind of green stuff that would presumably survive the cold now flanked her front door. Where had they come from?

"Clearly my cousin's been here." Reed, slid an arm around her waist. "That's got Cam written all over it."

"Awww. That's awfully nice of him. It makes the outside look almost like a real business."

"A closing day present. Ready to go in?"

Cecily held up her key. "Let's do it."

She unlocked the door and stepped inside, reaching for the light. "Why do I smell—oh my God."

Heart thumping, she took a few steps forward and stopped again. The place had not only been emptied, it'd been cleaned. The fresh scent of lemon oil hung in the air, punctuated by the incongruous scent of fresh biscuits. This, presumably, arose from the covered basket sitting on the desk. The *desk*. Across the vast space, a long, L-shaped desk was flanked by a pair of large bookcases. Cecily recognized Daniel's pallet-wood creations instantly. Across from them, a large markerboard on a rolling stand stood adjacent to an enormous bulletin board mounted on the back wall. The pair of vintage club chairs she'd been eying at Park Place created a nice seating area in front of the desk. Christoff's hand was visible in the bold grommet-top curtains flanking the windows.

She spied an envelope in the seat of the nice,

shiny new office chair. Tears pricked her eyes as she retrieved it.

Dear Cecily,

Happy closing day! We're so excited you've decided to stay and make your home here. You've been an enormous boon to us so we wanted to leave you a little welcome to get you started. Best of luck with your new business.

Norah, Cam, Christoff, Daniel, Beth, and Addison

"I'm going to cry," she said.

"Hold off on that a few more minutes," Reed told her. "I've got my own contribution." He reached behind the bookcase and pulled out a large frame. The Superman crest with a giant emblazoned C, painted in vintage comicbook style. "In case you ever start to doubt yourself."

On a watery laugh, Cecily threw her arms around his neck. "It's wonderful. You're wonderful." She rained kisses over his face.

Reed's arms tightened around her, and he tipped his mouth down to hers for a lingering kiss. "Glad you think so, but that's not it."

"What more can there be?"

"This whole venture is about you setting out on your own, going after the life, the work you want, on your terms. I couldn't be prouder of you. And you've inspired me to do the same."

Not understanding, Cecily shook her head. "But you've already gone after the work you want. Inglenook is well on the way to being that community hub."

"Entirely thanks to you. I have exactly what I want in work. Now it's time to go after what I want for the rest of my life."

"What's that?"

Taking her hand, he stepped back and dropped to one knee. "You."

"Ohmygod."

"A wise woman once told me, 'When you know, you know.' I knew you were it for me that night we went to Oxford. So, Cecily Davenport Dixon, will you marry me and make me a permanent part of this new life you're starting?"

She'd been the one to tell him that, when

she'd told him her parents' love story. And somewhere, deep down, she'd known, too. Because Reed had always seen beyond the surface to the real her.

Cecily dropped to her knees and took his other hand, bringing them both to her heart. "I wouldn't have it any other way."

~

Choose Your Next Romance!

Next up in the Wishful lineup, we return to the community theater crew. *Turn My World Around* basically came out of a dare from my editor to redeem former mean girl Corinne Dawson. This one is a must read for anybody who loves Dancing With The Stars!

Or maybe you'd like to see more of Reed's buddies. Zach Warren, our favorite photographer, finds his match in a second chance, friends to lovers romance that's ideal for fans of class reunion stories or anyone who has high school or prom trauma. Check out *Dancing Away With My Heart*!

And as an extra special bonus, I've also included *Once Upon A Coffee*, a Wishful Meet Cute Romance about Avery and Dillon!

ONCE UPON A COFFEE

A WISHFUL MEET CUTE ROMANCE

Professor Hendricks was a certifiable asshole. As Dillon Lange climbed the stairs to his second floor apartment, he ran through a number of other less than flattering descriptions for the man who didn't give a damn that Dillon's project partner had a ruptured appendix, thus blowing their chances of finishing the midterm project on time. At least if they expected to finish it together.

"You should've planned for this," Hendricks had said when Dillon met with him to plead for leniency since Noelle was still in the hospital.

Right, because a *ruptured organ* was so easy to predict. Noelle felt awful about leaving him in the lurch, but she was so doped up on medication, she could barely stay awake, let alone string a coherent sentence together. During his brief conversation with her about it, she'd fallen asleep twice and woken up with a lurch, shouting "Save the crazy cat lady!" Totally *not* the frame of mind they needed for a project on macroeconomics. Because Dillon wasn't an asshole himself, he'd said he'd take care of the project and that she should focus on getting well.

God, he missed undergrad when he could still live from class to nap to party.

The thump of machine gun fire greeted Dillon before he even got the door open.

Half crouched on the futon, half standing, his roommate Owen clutched the Xbox controller with all the intensity of a drone pilot on a mission as war raged on the flat screen TV. "Come *on,* dude! You've gotta close in on the flank, I'm getting slaughtered here!"

Battlefield? Titanfall? Hell if Dillon knew. He hadn't had time for video games since he started his MBA at the University of Mississippi. He was at *least* two editions of Assassin's Creed behind.

Owen grunted as Dillon shut the door. "Hey man. How'd it go?"

"Lousy." Dillon dumped his keys in the Cool Whip bowl that served as a catch all by the door. "No extension."

"That bites. No, no not you," he spoke into the headset perched in his shaggy dark hair. "Well, yeah, getting ambushed at the spawning point bites, too. I'm comin' to you. Hang on."

"Are you gonna be at this a while? Because I've got a crapton of work to do on this project if I'm going to make the deadline."

"Huh? Oh, well we're in the early stage of this campaign. I can't walk away right now."

Of course, he couldn't.

Heaving a put upon sigh that was completely lost on his roommate, Dillon made a beeline for his room. No way could he work here with all this noise. Loading up his laptop and all the books he'd need for this project, he retrieved his keys and headed downtown to hole up at his favorite coffee shop.

There was, predictably, no parking on the Square. Not a shock. The weather was gorgeous and sunny, and everybody in Oxford was out enjoying it. Couples and groups teemed like ants along the sidewalks. None of *them* had an epic midterm deadline hanging over their head. As he drove past Uptown Coffee, he saw patrons spilling out the doors, effectively squashing that plan. Hooking a left back toward campus, Dillon considered camping out at the library, but he needed caffeine to get through this. Gallons of it. He didn't want to have to pack up and relocate once he got set up.

This called for drastic measures.

Forty-five minutes later, Dillon rolled into the sleepy little town of Wishful. He'd stumbled upon this little jewel on one of his rambles in undergrad. Boasting a population of only 5,000, it reminded Dillon of his hometown in Texas.

Friendly, quirky, and, most importantly, *quiet,* it made Oxford look positively metropolitan in contrast.

As he pulled into a parking space in front of Lickety Split Ice Cream, a family of five wandered by, talking and laughing as they did their best to catch drips from their ice cream cones. Dillon gave fleeting thought to ice cream.

A reward when I finish, he decided. That presupposed it would be open when he finished. If that wasn't optimism, he didn't know what was.

Gathering his gear, Dillon walked the short distance to his actual destination. The Daily Grind was cool and dark and blessedly empty but for a pair of old guys playing checkers in the corner. Somebody was moving around in the kitchen at the end of the counter, so Dillon took the time to peruse the menu tacked up to the pallet board wall.

"Welcome to The Daily Grind. What can I get you?" The barista, a college-age guy with spiked, frosted blond hair, offered a flirty smile.

The name tag pinned to his purple apron read *Daniel.*

"Whatever you've got that will get me through an epic midterm deadline."

Daniel nodded soberly. "You want the zombie killer. Would you like anything to go with that? A muffin? Scone? Blueberry crumble bar?"

"Am I going to have any stomach lining left after drinking it if I don't?"

"Iffy. I'd soak some up with carbs."

"Then I'll have a slice of that friendship bread."

"Heated?"

"Sure."

The barista rang up his order. "Did you drive over from the university?"

"Yeah. Needed to get out of town to get some quiet so I could finish a project," said Dillon.

"You'll certainly get that here. I suggest you set up upstairs. You'll miss the afternoon rush that way."

"Is there much of a rush here?" Dillon couldn't imagine that in a town this size.

"Honey, you do *not* want to get between some of these soccer moms and their afternoon caffeine fix."

"Noted," Dillon chuckled.

"You go on up. I'll bring this when it's ready."

"Thanks."

The second floor of the coffeeshop was empty. Dillon picked a booth by a window and spread out his stuff. By the time Daniel brought his order, Dillon was already up to his eyeballs in Noelle's notes on her portion of the presentation. It was gonna be a long day.

Avery Cahill parked her faithful Toyota beside the town green and resisted the urge to wipe her damp palms on the legs of her capris. *Stupid to be nervous,* she thought. It was just coffee. And a more or less blind date with a guy she'd been matched up with on Perfect Chemistry. A guy with no profile picture.

He'd said he was camera shy—which could mean…anything. Actually shy. Physically deformed. Homely. Axe murderer. Her friends hadn't even thought she should talk to a guy not willing to put his picture up, but he'd seemed nice in their admittedly non-personal conversations. Respectful, which was something in astoundingly short supply in online dating. The things some guys thought they could get away with—insults, asking directly for booty calls, texting naked pictures of themselves—it had almost made her give up on online dating entirely.

But Ross had done none of those things. He'd been friendly and made no assumptions. They'd talked movies and TV and SEC football, steering clear of pretty much all things personal and identifying owing to that whole could-be-an-axe-murderer thing. She could get over the fact that he was a lifelong Bulldog fan. Probably. He was an architecture grad student at

Mississippi State, after all. She could get through a conversation with a guy who thought "Hail State!" was a more inventive battle cry than "Hotty Toddy!" It was worth a try, anyway. It wasn't as if the post-college dating scene in Wishful was exactly jumping. So when he'd said he was coming to town for the afternoon and suggested they meet for coffee, she'd said yes. Public place. Daytime. She'd get a better feel for him in person than from online anyway.

It wasn't a big deal.

So she'd changed her outfit. Twice. And gnawed off her lipstick and had to reapply. Avery had known that if she stayed home and thought about it any more, she'd end up over thinking and canceling on him. Or worse, standing him up because he'd already left Starkville and didn't get the message. So, she'd arrived early and decided to walk to The Daily Grind so there'd be time to get her nerves under control.

Sunlight filtered through the enormous oak trees that peppered the green, dappling the spotty grass. Summer had baked the ground in places, and the green hadn't quite recovered. In another month or two, the leaves would turn brown and fall—Mississippi rarely saw much in the way of autumn color—but for now, the green was as she liked it best. Bright and breezy.

Out of long ingrained habit, Avery stopped by the huge central fountain that dated back to the town's founding, just after the Civil War. She was pretty sure it hadn't run since she was little bitty, but her granddaddy had trained her to make a wish every time she walked by, and today was no exception. Clutching a coin in her hand, she thought, *I wish for this date to be something special.* Then she tossed it into the basin, where it plunked into the few inches of rainwater that hadn't evaporated over the summer. It was both tradition and comfort, and Avery felt some of the nerves smooth out.

Thus fortified by local ritual, Avery strode purposefully to The Grind. The date might be a disaster, but at least if the whole thing tanked, she'd have an entertaining story to tell around the water cooler at City Hall when she got to work on Monday.

"Well hey there, Sugarplum!"

The tension in Avery's shoulders immediately bled out at Daniel's cheery greeting.

"You're dressed up awful cute for an afternoon read-a-thon," he remarked, already turning to put together her current favorite Black Irish mocha.

"What?" She glanced down at the novel sticking out of her purse. "Oh...no. Actually, I'm here to meet somebody." She pulled out the book and the Gerbera daisy, clutching both to her chest.

Daniel arched both perfectly manicured brows. "Oh!" He drew the exclamation out to three syllables. "You're pulling a *You've Got Mail.* That's just adorable. Anybody I know?"

"Nobody *I* know. We got matched up on Perfect Chemistry. He's a grad student at the university."

Daniel brightened. "He's already here! Upstairs." He dropped his voice and leaned across the counter, offering her Black Irish. "A real hottie, too."

"Thank goodness," Avery sighed. "He didn't have a picture on his profile. Jessie was positive he had a third ear or weird mole or something. And Brooke was convinced he was a creeper."

"No strange growths or creepy vibes. Scout's honor," Daniel swore. "He's been working on a midterm project of some kind for a while now. Could probably do with a refill on his coffee. You want to take one up?"

"Sure." It would be a nice ice breaker.

Daniel made it up and handed over the second cup. "Good luck, cupcake. If he turns out to be a stinker, just text me an SOS and I'll create a diversion to get you loose."

"You're an angel."

Avery took the stairs slowly. With her luck, she'd step wrong in her wedge sandals and slosh coffee on her pale khaki capri pants in a highly embarrassing location. But she made it to the top with her outfit unmarred.

He was the only patron up here. Hunched over a laptop, with a stack of books and notes scattered on the table around him, she could just make out the strong edge of his jaw and the serious set to his mouth. Maybe he'd come early planning to get some homework out of the way before their date? Avery considered turning around and going back downstairs until the appointed time, just to give him a chance to finish what he was working on. Then he looked up and she almost bobbled the coffee.

Daniel hadn't exaggerated. This guy *was* a certifiable hottie with all that dark hair mussed by frustrated or nervous hands and those clear gray eyes that seemed to pierce her from across the room. His brows winged up in question.

Aware she was staring, Avery mustered a smile and crossed over, setting the cup of coffee in the few inches of free space beside the empty cup already there. "Daniel said you could do with a refill." She slid into the booth across from him and laid her book and flower next to her own coffee. "It's so nice to finally meet you."

As the brunette slid into the seat across the table, Dillon realized three things. One, she wasn't a waitress getting her flirt on. Two, it was really hard to be annoyed at being interrupted by a beautiful girl. Three, she completely thought he was somebody else.

"I'm so glad I'm not the only one who believes in showing up early." Freed of the coffees, her hands darted briefly, like hummingbirds unsure where to land, before settling in her lap.

Dillon recognized nerves when he saw them. He opened his mouth to tell her she'd made a mistake, then his eyes lit on the book she'd set between them. The latest in The Iron Druid Chronicles.

"You're a Kevin Hearne fan?" he asked.

Her eyes crinkled when she smiled, giving her a faintly feline look as she said, "Yes! Have you read this one?"

Dillon quickly held up a hand. "No. Don't say a word. I'm three books behind in the series and have been rabidly avoiding spoilers. I didn't discover them until *after* I started grad school, so there's not a lot of free time for reading."

"No, I imagine not. I confess, I've been a reading *machine* since I graduated two years ago. I haven't been able to get enough of all things commercial fiction. I'm sure my English professors would have a heart attack that I'm reading something other than Faulkner."

"And yet, you were an English major?" he asked.

"Honestly, it seemed like a good idea at the time. I like reading. They don't tell you when you sign up to major in English that what they do isn't *reading.* It's analyzing texts—often by a bunch of dead white guys that haven't been rel-evant in at least a century—to within an inch of their lives." She shuddered theatrically and sipped at her coffee. "I'm pretty sure they make up at least half of all the hidden meanings. I re-ally don't give a damn what the author suppos-edly meant by the curtains being blue. Sometimes, the curtains are just blue."

Dillon grinned. "Or the light at the end of the pier in Gatsby was just a green light."

"Yes!" She lifted her coffee in a gesture of agreement so enthusiastic, he expected it to slosh.

"Why didn't you switch majors?"

"Eh, I was already most of the way through. The alternatives would've involved adding a bunch of stuff and graduating later. I was ready to get *out*. Though I do miss having time for a daily nap."

"Naps are one of the greatest benefits of undergrad," Dillon agreed. "I'm pretty sure half the violence in the world would disappear if everybody had a daily nap. I know I'd be much less inclined to murder my roommate if I got one."

"I guess you don't much have time for that between juggling classes and your assistantship."

"Not so much, no." So whoever she was supposed to meet was also a grad student. He really *ought* to say something. But she looked so sweet as she absently played with the stem of the daisy, her attention focused on him. He could at least keep her company while she waited for her real date to show up. "So, what is it you do now with your English degree that doesn't offer a chance for a daily siesta?"

"I'm the city recorder and personal assistant to the mayor."

"City recorder. That sounds all official."

"I'm pretty sure I got the job because I can type accurately at over a hundred words per minute. Writing all those papers in college had that side benefit. Mostly I'm a gopher for whatever Sandra—Sandra Crawford is our mayor—needs me to do."

"Do you like it?"

She shrugged. "It keeps me busy. And I'm usually in on whatever drama results from small town politics, which can be very entertaining."

"Oh yeah? Like what?"

"Like..." She tipped her head in consideration and the sunlight from the window hit her hair, bringing out all the rich, warm undertones and making Dillon itch to touch it to see if it was as silky as it looked. "Last month Leonard Culpepper—he's the president of the local historical preservation society—went to war with Bernice Davies over her choice of paint color for the Victorian she's been restoring."

"What was wrong with the paint color?"

"Well, hot pink was definitely *not* historically accurate. It went all the way to the City Council."

"So what happened?"

"It turns out that Bernice is actually color blind. *She* thought the color she'd picked out was a kind of gray green. Never crossed her mind that 'razzle dazzle' didn't make much sense for a green. They've been warned down at the hardware store not to let her pick out paint without assistance."

"You like the small town life," he said. There was no question about it. Her expression was one of comfort and satisfaction with her place in this tiny world.

"I do. So many people grow up and they're hell bound and determined to get away from where they grew up. I was really happy to come back. I like the fact that I run into my third grade teacher at the grocery store or my best friend's parents at church on Sunday. Roots are important."

"I miss them." The words slipped out before he realized. But hell, it was true.

"Where are you from? Originally, I mean."

"Little bitty town in East Texas called Rango."

Her eyes crinkled again. "Like the lizard in the movie?"

"Exactly like. It's 'bout this size. Part of why I come over here once in a while is because Wishful reminds me of home."

"What would you be doing if you were there now instead of in school?"

"Working at the feed and farm supply probably. Running cattle on the side."

"That's a big jump from architecture."

Ah ha, so his mysterious competition—and

when had he started thinking of this girl's real date as competition?—was from MSU.

"Yeah, it is," he agreed. It was the truth, in a general sense.

"What do you do on a cattle ranch in the fall?" As her bottle green eyes sparkled, Dillon could see she was imagining a Hollywood version of a dude ranch.

"This time of year, we'd be baling hay for winter. Making sure the herd is up to date on immunizations and such. It's not glamorous by any means. Most folks who raise cattle have other jobs too. It's hard to make a living at that on its own anymore."

"My granddaddy raised dairy cattle forever, same as his daddy and granddaddy before him. But they had to close the dairy, before I was born. Now he farms. Soy. Corn. Cotton. It's all a tough business these days." She paused to sip. "So will you go home once you finish with grad school?"

Dillon shrugged. "I don't know. Depends on how things unfold, I guess. Where I wind up getting a job. Whether it's just me to think about or if I'm in a relationship when I finish." And where had *that* come from? "Lots of unknown variables. What about you? Are you settled here for good?"

She smiled into her coffee and glanced back up at him through sooty lashes. "I am until somebody worth leaving for catches my eye."

What on *earth* possessed her to say that?

As she looked down into her mug again, she caught a flash of Ross's smile. Oh, yeah. That was why. He had a great smile—an inviting curve of lips that made you feel like you were sharing some kind of juicy secret.

He made so much better an impression in person than he did online.

"Why didn't you have a picture up on your Perfect Chemistry profile?" She couldn't resist asking and hoped it wasn't a sensitive subject.

The oddest expression crossed his features. "It wouldn't have been me."

Huh. He hadn't struck her as much of a philosopher in their previous conversations. "Well, I guess we do tend to place too much importance on physical appearance."

"Why are you on one of those sites? You can't tell me you have trouble finding dates."

"Wishful is a little bitty pond, in case you haven't noticed. Of the guys here in my relative age bracket, I already dated half of them in high school. The other half are either married, dated friends of mine long enough that it would be weird, or they just don't ring my bell. We don't get a whole lot of new blood, as it were. I'm sure your hometown is the same."

"True," he agreed. "In a town that size, we had to revoke the whole no dating your friends' exes rule, otherwise nobody would've had anybody to date. Most folks either married their high school sweetheart or hoped to meet somebody in college."

"Exactly. And since I didn't do that while I

was at Ole Miss, online dating helps...cast a slightly wider net. And it's nice to theoretically have a system to match you up on *some* kind of criteria that suggests compatibility."

"You think an algorithm or whatever can actually do that?"

"Don't you?" she asked. He *was* on the same dating site, after all.

"I don't think it's a substitute for real, in person conversation. It might be able to match you with somebody based on—I don't know— similar values or movie tastes or political views. And, sure, maybe you end up hitting it off. But I don't think there's any true substitute for a chance meeting where you feel that indefinable spark with a complete stranger—and you know they won't stay a stranger for long."

The moment stretched between them, pulling taut with awareness and unspoken things. Avery felt her skin prickle and thought if she reached over to touch his hand right now, she'd feel a snap of electricity.

The thump of footsteps on the stairs broke

the spell. Avery glanced over to see an unfamiliar guy step into the room. Tall and exceptionally thin, he had a mug in one hand and what appeared to be a sketchpad in the other. She gave him a polite smile as he paused to survey the room, then moved to take a seat in a booth by the other window.

"Well, there's definitely something to be said for serendipity," Avery admitted. "Whether it's facilitated by outside sources or not." She thought about the wish she'd made in the fountain and smiled. Maybe the old fountain still worked after all.

Ross lifted his mug in a toast. "To serendipity."

Avery clinked her mug to his.

Conversation shifted back to books. They both had diverse tastes—she liked urban fantasy and romance, he liked sci-fi and more traditional fantasy—but there was sufficient crossover that they had plenty to discuss. Avery had to appreciate a man who could as readily debate George R. R. Martin's no character is safe policy as whether *The Hunger Games* was a reasonably accurate political forecast for the distant future. But she really knew she'd found someone special when he confessed to being one of the original backers of *The Veronica Mars Movie* and said he owned the entire series on DVD.

"Season one is as close to a perfect series of television as I've ever seen," he declared.

New guy checked his watch and fidgeted, tapping a pencil lightly against his sketchpad. The sound wasn't *quite* loud enough to be truly annoying. He looked nervous. *Waiting for somebody*, she guessed. Knowing very well how that felt, Avery silently wished him as much luck on his date as she was having on hers.

"Hey," said Ross, "I saw an ice cream parlor a bit down the street. How do you feel about banana splits?"

"They are one of the singular joys in life," said Avery. "Extra peanut butter?"

"Naturally."

"Then why don't we relocate," he said.

"I support this plan," she said. Ice cream was always a good idea.

Ross shut the laptop he'd shoved aside sometime during their conversation and began to gather up the notes scattered across the table. As he started to stuff his bag, Avery's attention strayed to the books he'd brought. A compulsive reader, she angled her head to get a better view of the titles. *Peddling Prosperity: Economic Sense and Nonsense in an Age of Diminished Expectations. The Return of Depression Economics.*

How odd, thought Avery. "Economics?" she asked. "Are you taking business classes on top of the requirements for your architecture degree? Doesn't that make you a glutton for punishment?

Ross stopped stuffing his bag and gave her a sheepish look. "Ah, about that."

"Excuse me." The newcomer stood by their table. "But are you Avery?"

Avery had a very bad feeling as she cautiously answered, "Yes."

"I'm Ross," he said, with a look that clearly

said Party Foul to her companion. "Your actual date."

Avery's face cycled through a number of different emotions—distress, embarrassment, maybe even disappointment—before she finally pinned him with a horrified glare. "You're not Ross?"

Dillon gave a *what-can-you-do?* shrug. "Guilty."

"Why didn't you say anything?" she demanded.

"You didn't ask," he said. Wrong answer.

She shot to her feet, hands fumbling for her book and coffee as she looked to her real date. "I'm so sorry for the confusion! I got here early and we simply don't get that many new faces in town. Daniel said—well it doesn't matter. We made assumptions. I thought he was you."

"No harm, no foul," said Ross, though the glance he shot back at Dillon suggested otherwise. "Shall we?" He gestured for her to precede him.

"Thanks for the coffee and conversation," said Dillon.

Avery made a little *hrmph* by way of reply. She left her daisy behind as she followed Ross.

He expected they'd head downstairs, but instead, they settled at a table on the far side of the room.

Well hell, thought Dillon. He'd certainly blown that. As soon as the other guy had come up the stairs, Dillon had suspected it was probably her real date. He'd had crazy idea that if he could just get her out of there…

What, he thought, *that she wouldn't be pissed when you told her the truth later? That she felt that spark, too?*

Cursing himself as an idiot, he began laying his notes back out. Break time was over, and he had plenty of work to keep him busy.

Avery looked over at him as he opened his laptop again, her eyes narrowed. At what? His effrontery at actually staying put while she had her date? He was here first. She was the one who'd interrupted *him,* with her smiles and enthusiasm and chatter about books and small town living. He had *work* to do. He could've been a complete jerk and sent her packing when she sat down, but no, he'd been *polite.* Conversational.

And interested, damn it.

Dillon's gaze strayed back to Avery. He couldn't hear their quiet conversation over the music that piped through the speakers, but she certainly wasn't as animated with Ross as she had been talking to him. She was nervous again. Beneath the edge of the table, her hands twisted in her lap. Her smile seemed a little strained around the edges.

Was that his fault? Had he made her feel even more awkward over that blind date than she already did? Dillon felt a prick of guilt at that. He hadn't intended to make things more difficult for her, just wanted to enjoy the chance circumstance that had brought her to his table.

It didn't matter. What was done was done and couldn't be taken back.

He had work to do. Determined to finish what he'd come here for, Dillon whipped his books back out, opened his files and did his best to focus on the task at hand. His grade and Noelle's were counting on it.

He lasted all of fifteen minutes. The damned flower sat there in his periphery, its bright orange petals taunting him, indirectly dragging his focus back to Avery.

She wasn't even *laughing.* What kind of a date couldn't at least make her chuckle to put her at ease?

Catching her glancing his way again, Dillon made a goofy face. One corner of her mouth twitched before she quickly shifted her attention back to Ross. The guy seemed to be recounting some incredibly detailed… something…with visual aids. He was drawing on the pad he'd brought, and Avery was struggling to look appropriately serious, nodding and interjecting the occasional question.

Those long, slim fingers tapped against her mug.

Dillon tucked the daisy behind his ear, laced both fingers under his chin, and batted his eyes at her in a wholly exaggerated fashion. Though she didn't look directly at him, he knew Avery could see him from the corner of her eye when she let loose one short bark of laughter that she quickly covered with a coughing fit.

"You okay?" asked Ross.

"Yeah, yeah. I just swallowed wrong. Please, go on." Eyes on her date, Avery made a shooing motion at Dillon from beneath the table.

He smothered a grin behind one of the books.

You are a bad bad boy, he thought.

Vowing to behave, he turned his attention back to the computer screen and pretended to work for a few minutes, weaving Noelle's notes in with his own and making notations about where he needed to expand points with support from the class texts.

This whole situation needed musical accompaniment. Something other than the low key jazz favored by the coffee shop. Dillon dug through his eclectic and extensive music collection until he found what he was looking for. *Yes, this will do very nicely.* He hit *play* and Celine Dion belted out the chorus to "All By Myself" loud enough to echo off the high raftered ceiling.

Avery and her date both turned toward him with *WTF?* expressions.

"Sorry! Sorry." Dillon plugged his headphones into the correct port on his laptop and managed not to laugh. *The devil made me do it.*

Avery laid a hand over Ross's and gave him the first genuine smile Dillon had seen her muster since she left his table. "You wanna get out of here?"

Ross looked over his shoulder at Dillon again. "Sounds like a great idea."

Jealousy was an ugly shade of green.

They rose and headed for the stairs.

Look back, thought Dillon. *C'mon, look back at me.*

But Avery never turned as she descended from view. The last thing Dillon heard her say was something about an example of antebellum architecture she thought Ross might like to see. Then they were gone and his window of opportunity slammed closed for good.

"—and then he walks up and says *he's* my date. I've been sitting there for *forty-five minutes* talking to this guy and he never said a *word* to correct my assumption. It was *mortifying*." Avery's footsteps thudded against the stairs for emphasis as she climbed toward the third floor of City Hall.

Brooke slurped her to go cup of sweet tea. "What did your actual date say?"

"He was remarkably cool about the whole thing. Really polite. Which is more than I can say for Mr. Fake Date. We're sitting across the room, trying to get through all that initial blind date awkwardness, which was completely made worse by my gaffe, and the guy is making faces behind Ross's back. Ross was giving this completely earnest explanation of some architectural history thing, and it was all I could do not to fall over laughing."

"There are worse things than a man who can make you laugh," Brooke observed.

"Not when you're on a date with *somebody else*," Avery insisted. "I tried my best to cover, but I'm sure Ross thought I was the rudest thing ever. I finally just suggested that we go somewhere else, just to get away from him."

"And did that actually make the date with Ross the architect go better?"

Avery grimaced. "No. I might could've gotten past the multi-generation Bulldog legacy if we had a lick of chemistry or mutual interests, but bless his heart, once we blew past all the mutual pop culture references, we had absolutely nothing in common. He didn't even try to kiss me. I doubt I'll be hearing from him again." And that was a relief. This way she didn't have to find a way to turn him down gently.

"Probably just as well," Brooke said. "Lack of creeper vibe aside, I still don't trust a guy who wouldn't put his profile picture up. At least the day wasn't a total loss. It sounds like your fake date went better. You must've had *something* in common to chat for almost an hour without things getting weird."

We had tons in common, thought Avery with no little prick of regret. "Like that matters. I don't know his name or where he's a student or even what the heck he was *doing* here." And if she'd wondered for half a minute whether the yearbook photos from Rango, Texas were somewhere online, she'd quickly put the thought out of her mind. She was *not* going to embarrass herself further by trying to track him down.

Avery and Brooke stepped into the reception area of the mayor's office to find a courier juggling a vase full of flowers.

"Can I help you?" Avery asked.

"Oh good. I'm not supposed to leave these without a signature," he said. Setting the flowers on her desk, the courier offered her a clipboard. "Just sign at the bottom."

Avery scribbled her signature. "I hope you haven't been waiting long. We tend to get kind of scarce around lunch."

"Enjoy," he said, and disappeared down the hall.

The mix of cream tulips and bright Gerbera daisies was unusual and happy. "Cam must've sent his mom flowers," Avery said. "He's such a sweetheart. Always doing stuff like that."

Insatiably curious, Brooke peered at the name on the card envelope. "These aren't for Mayor Crawford. They're for you."

"What? Who'd be sending me flowers?" She crossed over to pluck the card from the holder and eased it out.

Let me make it up to you. Tosca. Tuesday at 7 PM.

Avery's mouth dropped open.

Brooke looked over her shoulder. "It isn't signed."

Avery flipped the card over to verify, but no, it wasn't signed. The florist was out of Oxford.

"You've got a secret admirer," Brooke sang. "Kind of a strange combination of flowers."

"Cream tulips are for apology," Avery murmured.

The flowers had to be from her fake date. She'd never told Ross where she worked and he'd never seen the Gerbera daisy she'd brought. She'd forgotten it at Mr. Fake Date's table. A flutter of excitement trembled in her chest.

"They're from *him* aren't they?"

She didn't have to ask which him Brooke meant. "I think they must be."

"And he's asking you out! Properly. With style, I might add. Flowers that must've cost a pretty penny to deliver this far from Oxford. A dinner invite to the nicest restaurant in town. Are you going to go?"

"I don't know."

"Oh come on," Brooke said. "This is, like, the ultimate form of flattery. He *liked* you."

Avery didn't deny she was flattered. He'd remembered details, made an effort because he actually wanted to see her again. And there *had* been that moment, that serendipitous spark before the real Ross had showed up.

Yet…she hadn't gotten past the annoyance and embarrassment over what had happened at The Grind. How long would he have gone on lying to her if they hadn't been interrupted?

"How can I trust a guy who had multiple opportunities to come clean about not being my date and chose not to say anything?"

"He owns his bad behavior on the card and apologized with the flowers," insisted Brooke. "That's gotta earn some brownie points toward paying off the deficit."

"Are brownie points even a thing when you're not in a relationship?"

"You're avoiding the issue," Brooke insisted. "Worst case scenario, you get a nice dinner and a chance to ream him out for his behavior on

Saturday. Best case scenario, you find out who it is you *really* made a connection with. Isn't it worth going to find out which one?"

By ten after seven, Dillon was certain Avery wasn't going to show. He couldn't really blame her if she didn't. From her perspective, he'd lied. And then he'd deliberately gone about distracting her from her real date like some adolescent nut job.

Classy, dude.

Why had that seemed like a good idea? Class clown wasn't exactly a selling point for a mature relationship. Not that he'd given a lot of thought to looking for a mature relationship before now.

Once he'd turned in his project on Monday —after two almost all nighters—he still hadn't been able to get Avery out of his head. He knew he'd behaved badly, and his mama had raised him to apologize for bad behavior, so before he crashed, he went in search of a florist who was willing to deliver all the way to the Wishful City Hall. The gesture was a Hail Mary, and he wasn't sure what he hoped to accomplish by talking her into dinner. He just... wanted another shot at making a better first impression.

Too bad life didn't give you do overs on those.

He'd already unwrapped his silverware and drained his water glass—which did absolutely nothing to whet his parched mouth—when Avery appeared at the hostess station, looking gorgeous and...not entirely pleased to be there. Nerves and something like hope bumped up beneath his breastbone.

On his feet in an instant, Dillon rounded the table to pull out a chair as she crossed to him in a light blue dress and a pair of tall, strappy shoes that drew his eye unerringly to her well-toned legs.

Behave, he ordered himself.

"I didn't think you were coming," he said.

She gave him a long look with those catlike green eyes. "I almost didn't."

"Then I thank you for changing your mind." He gestured to the chair, and after a moment's hesitation, she sat.

Dillon's hand brushed her bare shoulder as he pushed in the chair, and he felt the zing of it up the whole length of his arm.

Don't screw this up.

The waiter appeared for Avery's drink order. Dillon took the fact that she ordered a glass of chardonnay as a sign that maybe she meant to stay. Or maybe she just wanted something with a little bite to toss in his face.

When they were alone again, she said, "Was anything you told me actually true?"

Dillon didn't hesitate. "All of it."

She lifted one dark brow in askance.

"I never lied to you, Avery. You just showed up and sat down and started talking."

"And you managed to talk back for almost an hour without mentioning that I'd made a mistake."

"I'll own that. But you're interesting and beautiful and I didn't want you to leave. So I might have sidestepped the truth to avoid lying."

She didn't soften at his feeble attempt at charm. "Is that supposed to make me feel better?"

"Just telling it like it is. You started the whole thing when you brought me coffee."

"That was all Daniel's doing."

If this worked out, Dillon totally owed the barista a beer or something.

"Nevertheless, a wise man doesn't turn away a beautiful woman with delicious stimulants. Even if he did have a behemoth group project he had to finish by himself on a deadline."

"Is that why you were there that day?"

"My roommate was surgically attached to the Xbox. I needed some quiet, so I came down here to work. Or try to work. Then you showed up."

"You could've said so."

"I thought about it for about thirty seconds.

But you were way more appealing than theories of macroeconomics. You didn't ask who I was, and by the time I realized you thought I was somebody else, I was enjoying our conversation. Something I hope we'll be able to do tonight. Unless," he added, "things went awesome with your real date over the weekend and you're just here out of pity."

Her lip began to tremble, and for a long, horrible moment, Dillon was afraid she might cry. Both arms wrapped around her middle, she bent double, her shoulders beginning to shake.

Oh God, what did I say wrong?

A burst of sound escaped. She slapped a hand over her mouth, eyes going wide. Then she was laughing, wincing, unable to stop as she said, "Oh my God, it was awful. And you were just sitting over there deliberately provoking me. What was I supposed to do?"

Dillon gave her a sheepish smile. "Sorry about that. I couldn't help myself. We'd been having such a good conversation and then you looked so...awkward with him."

"That's kind of a rule with blind dates."

"It wasn't with us," he pointed out. "There wasn't a single lull in *our* conversation."

"We didn't have a date," she clarified, pokering up. "We had an…encounter."

Warming to the debate, Dillon argued, "We had beverages and conversation. I say that qualifies as a date."

"It was a pseudo date," she allowed.

"Well then," he said, "let's see if we can do better on the real thing."

"On one condition."

Dillon resisted the urge to pump his fist in victory. "Name it, milady."

"We start with the important things. Like your *actual* name."

He grinned and offered his hand. "Dillon Lange."

She finally smiled as she reached across the table to take it. "Avery Cahill. It's nice to meet you."

Copyright 2014 Kait Nolan

- *Those Sweet Words* (Pru and Flynn)
- *Stay A Little Longer* (Athena and Logan)
- *Bring It On Home* (Maggie and Porter)

RESCUE MY HEART SERIES
SMALL TOWN MILITARY ROMANCE

- *Baby It's Cold Outside* (Ivy and Harrison)
- *What I Like About You* (Laurel and Sebastian)
- *Bad Case of Loving You* (Paisley and Ty prequel)
- *Made For Loving You* (Paisley and Ty)

MEN OF THE MISFIT INN
SMALL TOWN SOUTHERN ROMANCE

- *Let It Be Me* (Emerson and Caleb)
- *Our Kind of Love* (Abbey and Kyle)

WISHFUL SERIES

SMALL TOWN SOUTHERN ROMANCE

- *Once Upon A Coffee* (Avery and Dillon)
- *To Get Me To You* (Cam and Norah)
- *Know Me Well* (Liam and Riley)
- *Be Careful, It's My Heart* (Brody and Tyler)
- *Just For This Moment* (Myles and Piper)
- *Wish I Might* (Reed and Cecily)
- *Turn My World Around* (Tucker and Corinne)
- *Dance Me A Dream* (Jace and Tara)
- *See You Again* (Trey and Sandy)
- *The Christmas Fountain* (Chad and Mary Alice)
- *You Were Meant For Me* (Mitch and Tess)
- *A Lot Like Christmas* (Ryan and Hannah)
- *Dancing Away With My Heart* (Zach and Lexi)

WISHING FOR A HERO SERIES (A WISHFUL SPINOFF SERIES)
SMALL TOWN ROMANTIC SUSPENSE

- *Make You Feel My Love* (Judd and Autumn)
- *Watch Over Me* (Nash and Rowan)
- *Can't Take My Eyes Off You* (Ethan and Miranda)
- *Burn For You* (Sean and Delaney)

MEET CUTE ROMANCE
SMALL TOWN SHORT ROMANCE

- *Once Upon A Snow Day*
- *Once Upon A New Year's Eve*
- *Once Upon An Heirloom*
- *Once Upon A Coffee*
- *Once Upon A Campfire*
- *Once Upon A Rescue*

SUMMER CAMP
CONTEMPORARY ROMANCE

- *Once Upon A Campfire*
- *Second Chance Summer*

ABOUT KAIT

Kait is a Mississippi native, who often swears like a sailor, calls everyone sugar, honey, or dar-lin', and can wield a bless your heart like a saber or a Snuggie, depending on requirements.

You can find more information on this

RITA ® Award-winning author and her books on her website http://kaitnolan.com. While you're there, sign up for her newsletter so you don't miss out on news about new releases!